ISABELLA MINE

ISABELLA MINE

HELEN REEDER CROSS

ILLUSTRATED BY
CATHERINE STOCK

Lothrop, Lee & Shepard Books
New York

Library of Congress Cataloging in Publication Data
Cross, Helen Reeder.   Isabella Mine.
Summary: Eleven-year-old Molly finds life in a small community
in East Tennessee's Copper Basin to be full of activities and
adventures. [1. Family life—Fiction. 2. Mountain life—Fiction.
3. Tennessee—Fiction] I. Stock, Catherine, ill. II. Title.
PZ7.C8826Is   [Fic]   81-12346
ISBN 0-688-00885-2   AACR2

First Edition
1 2 3 4 5 6 7 8 9 10

For Fan and Nola
who also remember
Big Frog Mountain
and Little Potato Creek

CONTENTS

ISABELLA MINE

MOLLY'S MOUNTAINS

Molly sat hugging her knees on the front porch steps. Behind her, through open windows, she could hear Ruthie practising scales. Her middle sister's fingers were like butterflies on the keys. It was time for Molly's turn at the piano, but she didn't mean to go in yet. Not until the golden ball of the sun disappeared behind Big Frog Mountain.

"*My* mountain," Molly called it, for it was her favorite. Big Frog was the giant of a large circle of Great Smoky Mountains in East Tennessee. These lay trunk to tail, Molly liked to imagine, like quiet elephants rimming the Copper Basin. Isabella Mining Camp, her home, was in the middle of the Basin's bowl.

Elephants, as everybody knows, are always gray. But Big Frog "elephant" changed color with the weather's whim, or the time of day. It could be the green of its forest blanket or as blue as a jay's wing. Sometimes it deserved the name "Smoky." Now and then it hid completely behind black storm clouds.

Today Big Frog was deep purple. Above its rim the early evening sky was like the glow from the copper furnaces a mile away.

Molly began to imagine the other side of the world, where the sinking sun would spend the night. Perhaps there a cheerful giant would bounce the sun-ball all night long to his heart's content. Tomorrow he would toss it over the top of Angelico Mountain in the East, to light the Copper Basin for another day.

Suddenly Molly laughed at herself. She scooped up Puff, who came leaping softly up the steps, meowing for attention.

"What would Kate think if she knew about my giant with the sun-ball?" she asked herself. She didn't need to wonder. She knew exactly what her best friend would say. Molly could almost hear her now.

"Grow up, Molly Meade! You're eleven years old, going on twelve. Too old for fairy tales. Come on. Catch! This ball is *real!*"

Then she would throw an old tennis ball straight at Molly, just to see her miss it. Kate always had a ball in her pocket, ready for a quick game. Her head was stuffed with facts, not fancies. She had no patience with Molly's daydreams.

"I don't care what Kate thinks," Molly told herself now. She brushed Puff from her lap, for her left leg had a crick in it. She stood up and pulled down her middy blouse. "My giant and the sun-ball will be a good story to tell Penny. Then maybe she won't make me sing that old 'Baby's Boat' anymore. When I was four, I'm sure nobody had to sing lullabies to me."

Just then the piano scales stopped. Ruth came to the front door. She mashed her nose against the screen.

"Your turn, Molly," she said. "I practised thirty-seven whole minutes."

Her big sister was impressed. Thirty-seven minutes was a long time for a nine-year-old to sit still on a piano bench.

Molly pulled up her right knee sock, the one with the weak garter, and went indoors. At the piano bench she stacked Ruth's scattered music in a neat pile. Then she opened her own book of *Czerny Finger Exercises*. Miss Julie was strict about warming up fingers before playing pieces. It was boring to play the same pages over and over, five times each. Still, Molly had found that she could think of other things at the same time.

Today her fingers raced each other up and down the keyboard, while her thoughts buzzed like a swarm of angry bees. It was Kate again. Miss Julie's piano recital for "the young ladies and gentlemen of Isabella Camp" was just a week away. Kate's piece was a showy "Mexican Hat Dance." Molly's was called "Romance."

"You must play your 'Romance' with great expression," Miss Julie had said at yesterday's music lesson. "I chose it for you, dear, because you have a sensitive touch."

Molly sniffed, remembering. Who cares about a sensitive touch? "Romance" was soft and sweet. It sounded easy as pie. No one would ever guess how hard she had worked to learn all those arpeggios and trills. "Mexican Hat Dance" was Kate's kind of music—splashy, fast as lightning, and loud. Everybody would gasp at her cleverness.

Sometimes I hate that Kate! Molly thought angrily. Hate-Kate; Kate-hate! It was like a witch's spell. Today Molly liked the ugly rhyme.

Just then her fingers tangled in a muddled discord. She was a little ashamed. After all, wasn't Kate her best friend? Not that there was anybody else to be best friends with. She and Kate were the only sixth graders at Isabella School. The other thirteen children, all with fathers who were officials of the Copper Company, were younger—only babies, really. Just the same, sometimes it was hard not to hate Kate.

"Supper's ready!" Mother called. Supper was family time. Tonight Ruthie had an "A" in arithmetic to crow about. Jenny dropped her bread on the floor, butter side down, only once. That was good for a four-year-old. There were chicken and dumplings—Vashti's best dish, Mother often said. And brown betty for dessert. Molly had made the hard sauce, sprinkled with lots of nutmeg. As usual, Ruth and Penny begged for more sauce than pudding.

"I'm glad we're growing a young cook in the family," Daddy said, smiling at Molly. "Now we won't starve if Vashti develops a toothache and takes the train back to Atlanta."

"As if I couldn't cook!" Mother pouted, making a face at him. "I'm tempted not to tell any of you my surprise."

"Tell us! Tell us! Please!" the children pleaded. So Mother did.

"I had a letter today. We're going to have company.

Cousin Eva is coming to spend October in Isabella—to visit us and to see our mountains. Can you believe it? In her whole life Cousin Eva has never seen a mountain. She lives in flatlands, with not even a hill for a hundred miles."

Ruthie's blue eyes opened wide. So did Molly's. In their whole lives they had almost never been out of sight of mountains.

"Besides that," Daddy said, pushing back his chair and lighting his pipe, "I'll bet my buttons Eva's never been down in a copper mine. We'll arrange a few surprises for her, won't we?" He tickled Ruth's bare knee under the tablecloth to make her jump, then winked at Molly. "On second thought, we'd better wait and see. Lady poets like your Cousin Eva might not like going into the dark world underground. From what I hear, lady poets like sunshine and bluebirds and roses."

"She certainly likes parties," Mother said. "When Eva and I were girls, there was nothing in all the world we liked as well as parties."

Penny began to bounce up and down. She almost slipped off the two dictionaries that kept her chin out of her plate.

"Pink ice cream parties, Mommy? I like pink ice cream," she crowed and clapped her chubby hands. "I like cakes with candles to blow out, too."

"Silly! Grown-ups don't want ice cream at their parties. Or candles either," Ruth told her. She picked up Penny's spoon, which had fallen on the floor. "Maybe Cousin Eva would like a picnic at our best spot, on Hairpin Bend, with watermelon for dessert."

"There aren't any watermelons in October," Molly squelched her sister. Just the same she was excited, too. Company in the house for a whole month—even grown-up company—meant all sorts of fun and surprises for children, too.

As soon as dinner was over, she dashed to the telephone to call Kate.

"I know some news you don't know," she told her sometimes-enemy, sometimes-best friend. "You'll never guess it in a million years."

"I already know about your Cousin Eva," Kate said smugly. "Your mother told my mother all about her at bridge club this afternoon. I know she's coming for a visit."

Molly felt like a balloon pricked with one of Mother's

hat pins. But then Kate made things better. Sometimes she could be sweet, and she often had daring ideas.

"Tomorrow's Saturday," Kate said. "Let's explore somewhere we've never been." Then she whispered hoarsely into the phone, "Let's cross Little Potato Creek where there's no bridge and hike down the Old England Road. We won't tell a soul where we're going. I don't believe those stories about bootleggers hiding in the hills, do you?"

So Molly went to sleep that night with two good things to think about. One was Cousin Eva's visit; the other was the secret exploring expedition down Old England Road. Mother would object. So would Kate's mother, if they knew. Sometimes it was better not to ask. Then the answer wouldn't be no. She and Kate would be careful. After all, weren't they both eleven years old, almost twelve?

2

EXPLORING GULLIES

It was a beautiful morning for a secret expedition. Today there were no tag-along little sisters, either. Because Mother was hemming her recital dress, Ruth must stay home to try it on. So Ruth was now making sand tarts with Penny in the sand pile. Kate had two little sisters and a baby brother (besides a big sister, Josie, who was in Ducktown High School). Molly wondered how Kate had managed to escape taking care of the younger ones on a Saturday morning.

Molly had already practised for forty-five minutes after breakfast. She had fed the rabbits their limp lettuce leaves and carrot tops from last night's supper. She had cleaned her room like a whirlwind.

Her most important Saturday job was making the family's weekly jar of mayonnaise. This could wait until afternoon, while Vashti rested and the kitchen was empty. Making mayonnaise wasn't really a chore. It was fun to watch dribbled oil thicken the two egg yolks. She whirled the beater until her right arm ached. It seemed a kind of kitchen magic. Besides, Molly loved tasting the mayonnaise now and then, to test its lemony tartness.

"Mother, Kate and I are going for a walk," Molly called now. She slipped quickly out the back door before anyone could think of a reason for stopping her.

The two girls met at the back gate. Molly shut it carefully, to keep it from squeaking. Suddenly she and Kate were conspirators. Molly glanced at the kitchen window. It would spoil everything if Vashti saw them turn down Old England Road. Children of Isabella Camp were never allowed to walk there. It wound among the hills where scattered mountain people lived —out of sight of camp mothers. It was a rule of Isabella mothers always to know, and usually to see, where their children were playing.

Once past the second bend in the road, the girls were out of sight from Molly's house. Molly's heart slowed down.

"This is fun," Kate said. She did a little turkey trot step or two in the middle of the dusty road. "Forbidden things are always fun. I wonder why." She pulled a plume of broomsedge grass and bit its juicy stem thoughtfully. It tasted a little bitter, a little sweet.

"You don't believe the story about bootleggers living down this road, do you?" Molly asked. "I wouldn't want to meet one, would you? If we did, what do you suppose he'd look like?"

"Don't be silly!" Kate said scornfully. "He'd look just like anybody else, only he might be drunk."

Molly changed the subject.

"It hasn't rained for a week," she said, "so it ought to be easy to cross Little Potato Creek on foot, don't you think? I guess if cars and wagons can ford it, so can we."

Little Potato Creek was an old friend. It began somewhere high in the mountains. Here it ran gently through a flat flood plain. The creek divided Isabella Camp, whose copper company houses clung to hills on either side. Molly and Kate crossed it on a narrow foot-

bridge every day, to and from Isabella School. Farther down, near the copper furnaces, there was a wider bridge for cars.

Molly was right. Today the water of the creek sparkled shallowly in the sun. The girls were tempted to look for crawdads and pieces of quartz in the clear water. But they could do that any old time. This was Exploring Day.

They jumped gingerly from stone to stone. It would be too bad to get wet feet so early in the hike. Beyond the creek the road curved around another hill. This was now strange country.

This side of the hill had many more clumps of broomsedge grass. It grew in patches, like dry islands. Now, in September, the coarse grass was tall and feathery—tall enough to hide in. A gentle wind blew it in waves like the sea, Molly thought. Or like the silvery hair of an old man. Someday she would write a poem about broomsedge. About how it looked like silk but was really tough and scratchy to touch. Some people were like that.

The other side of the hill, the one nearest Isabella, had matched other hills of the Copper Basin with hardly any grass and never a bush or tree. Here, the clay was scarred with gullies, like the wrinkled skin of an old apple. After a rain the clay was bright red. In dry weather, like today, it turned a faded pink. Under melting snow, Molly thought the clay hillsides looked like devil's food cakes with runny white frosting in the cracks.

"Let's explore that gully." Kate pointed to a deep gash in the hill's surface. It was wide at the foot of the hill and, like all gullies, narrowed at its top.

Exploring gullies was the best of games. Copper Basin children played it daily in many forms, just outside the fences of their own front yards. Hide-and-Seek, Indian Raids, Prospecting for Gold. There was no end to the possibilities. Here was a new gully, so far unexplored. Who could tell what it might lead to? So Molly and Kate plunged into it and began to climb.

At first the gully's sides towered steeply over their heads. With every step the girls looked closely at the bare pink clay on either side. Being Isabella children, they always did this, hoping to find treasure.

Sometimes the treasure was an arrowhead. Sometimes, if the hunter was lucky, it might be a piece of quartz, milky white or rose-colored. Now and then treasure seekers found whole garnets, half-buried in a loose rock. Captain Jim, the mine captain, knew how to polish these into shining jewel shapes, deep red like drops of blood. Molly longed to find a perfect garnet someday and have it set in a ring. Garnet was her birthstone.

Today, of course, it was Kate who found an arrowhead. Her collection was already the best of anybody's at Isabella School.

"Your eyes are sharper than mine," Molly admitted generously. She was a little envious. Still, she had to admire the perfect shape of the tiny arrowhead. It had been chiseled so long ago by an Indian hunter. Its point was still sharp enough to kill a deer—if any had been left to roam the hills. But deer had vanished from the Copper Basin long ago.

At last the gully petered out. Here it was narrow enough to jump from side to side, which for a while the girls did. Kate could jump at the widest spots. Perhaps her legs were longer, Molly thought, though the girls were exactly the same height.

Then they were on the crest of the hill. Both gasped. What a sight! Below and behind them in the distance they could see Little Potato Creek. It wound its lazy, crooked way through Isabella Camp, which looked from here like a village of toy blocks.

"I can see your house with the green roof," Kate said, pointing, "but not mine. It's hidden behind that hill to the right."

"There's Isabella School," Molly said, "and the clubhouse. I can count five houses from here: the McFees', the Fryes', the Bradfords', ours, and the Millers'." There was a cloud of burnt orange smoke in the distance. "That smoke is from the copper furnaces."

"Look!" Kate exclaimed. "There's a car. It looks like a wind-up toy, climbing on a track instead of a cinder road."

It was strange to see home from such a height and distance.

"I feel like a giant, don't you?" Molly asked, remembering her sun-ball story. She had not told Kate about her giant. "We're surveying our kingdom from an invisible castle tower."

"Except we're not invisible," Kate remarked. "We can see your house from here, so somebody there can see us, if they look this way."

Trust Kate to be practical. She was right. The two girls dropped to the ground in a patch of broomsedge and hoped they hadn't been seen. They gazed into the distance. The faraway circle of green mountains surrounded them. It was like a rim around a bowl of wrinkled pink clay hills.

"Can you imagine the time when the Copper Basin was covered with trees?" Kate asked. "When it was the Cherokee Indians' hunting ground? Before the white man discovered copper under the forests?"

"It's hard to imagine," Molly admitted. She knew the story; everybody did. Almost a hundred years ago the copper had been smelted in open-air furnaces. Strong fumes from the molten metal had killed the thick forest for many miles around. Trees—great pines and oaks and chestnuts—had slowly rotted and been washed away. Rains had worn gullies into bare hills. Now there were no trees left, not one for many miles. Here and there a patch of broomsedge, like this one, was trying to find a roothold. Nothing else could grow in the starved clay, except a few stray cactus plants with yellow blossoms guarded by spines.

"Come on!" Kate said, jumping up. "Let's explore some more. I'll race you to the foot of the hill."

So the girls zigzagged their way back down to Old England Road.

"I have an idea," Kate said, as they scuffed through the deep dust. Here the road's slag surface had petered out. Few cars and wagons used it, so no one had bothered to keep the road in repair. Today the girls had passed no one at all.

"There's a country church around the next bend," Kate continued. "It's where the mountain people go. I saw it once when I went with my daddy to take old Mrs. Corn home to her cabin. It was her day to scrub for us. It was raining hard, and she was half-sick. Too sick to walk. That mean old husband of hers was probably drunk somewhere. We felt sorry for her."

"I've heard her talk about her church," Molly said. "She's terribly proud of it. She says it has a real organ; and the preacher comes there every six weeks, even in winter. I like to talk with Mrs. Corn, poor old thing. Sometimes when she scrubs for my mother, I sit at the kitchen table just to hear her stories. I don't really believe it, but she says she remembers the Civil War. That would make her be about seventy-five years old. I don't know anybody as old as that, do you?"

"She's that old, I'm sure," Kate laughed. "It would take that many years for her to grow so crooked and wrinkled."

Molly said nothing to this. She was fond of the old mountain woman and felt sorry for her all the time, not just some of the time. Mrs. Corn had that mean old husband and a "passel" of ungrateful grown children, who never did anything nice for her. At her age she shouldn't have to scrub floors for Isabella ladies. Besides, she had had a lot of sadness in her long life. Once she had told Molly about her favorite child who had died long ago. Molly could even remember her words.

"I'm still a-payin' that funeral man ten cents a week for Johnny's tombstone," she had said, cracking her broken teeth on a chicken bone as she spoke. "That tombstone is the purtiest thing a body ever seen. I writ a pome to go on it, a long time ago."

Sometime Molly would like to see that gravestone.

3

LITTLE JOHNNY'S GRAVE

Sure enough, the tiny church was just around the next bend of the road. It had once been white. Now most of its paint had peeled off, leaving bare boards. There was a fat belfry with no bell. Over the sagging door was the name "Hopewell Gospel Church." Behind the church, straggling up the hillside, lay a topsy-turvy cemetery.

The door, of course, was locked, but the windows were low. Molly and Kate, by standing on tiptoe, could look inside.

"There's the organ!" Molly exclaimed. "It's the old-fashioned parlor kind, like the one in my Aunt Sally's attic. I wish we could play it."

"Let's try," said Kate. Behind the church she found a rickety wooden box. By standing on it and moving it from window to window, the girls found one unlocked.

"Come on!" Kate dared. "Let's climb inside. We won't hurt anything. We'll just try that organ."

"Do you think we should?" Molly asked timidly. But Kate was already halfway through the open window. Molly followed. Her heart thumped loudly enough, she was sure, to be heard a mile away.

Inside the church was dusty and almost bare. There were only a pulpit that looked like an upended woodbox and a few rows of plain pews. A worn green hymnbook lay open on the music rack.

"It's the kind of organ that has to be pumped with your feet," Kate said. She examined it closely. "I bet it's hard to move your feet and fingers at the same time. I'll try it."

She slid onto the organ bench and tried out a few measures of "Gypsy Dance" from memory. At a hard spot in the music, she forgot to pump the pedals. The wheezy organ sounds stopped dead in the middle of a note.

"Suppose somebody hears us," Molly said. "What would we do?"

"Scaredy-Cat!" Kate said. "How many people travel on Old England Road? Nobody lives way out here, back in the hills, unless maybe a bootlegger or two. And they don't know much about organs, I bet. What's more, they've probably never been inside a church."

Molly ran to look out the window. Not a soul was in sight.

"Now it's my turn to play," she said firmly. "I can sightread some of these hymns." She turned the musty pages of the hymnal to number 30. Its name was "Roll On, Jordan, Roll."

Reading music at sight was one thing she could do better than Kate, she knew. She found it easy as pie to push the pedals evenly, one after the other, while her fingers pressed the stiff keys. The sound that came from the old instrument was quavery and hoarse. It was scarcely music at all. But it was fun to play, like a new wind-up toy at Christmas.

Now Kate was beginning to be nervous.

"Come on," she urged. "We'd better go before somebody finds us. Mountain people are quick on their feet and quiet, like Indians. Some of them *are* part Cherokee. We might not hear them coming. They wouldn't like it that we broke into their church."

"What do you suppose they'd do to us?" Molly asked.

"Call the sheriff maybe," Kate said. "Then we *would* be in trouble. I've seen the sheriff on the street in Ducktown. He wears a gun in his belt."

It took only a minute to slip out the window, shut it tightly, and set the box back where they had found it. There was still no one on the road.

"While we're here," Molly said, breathing quietly again, "let's look at some of the tombstones in the cemetery. I've never been in a cemetery before, have you?" She was a little surprised at her own daring.

The graveyard was a neglected little plot of ground. There was not one bush or tree. Graves were scattered over the red clay hillside. Islands of broomsedge, like uncut hair, separated them. Only a few of the graves had stones, and most of these sagged crookedly. Heavy rains had washed small gullies here and there.

Some of the newer graves had glass fruit jars half-set into the ground. In a few of these, there drooped faded yellow, red, and pink paper roses, with curled petals and green wire stems. Mountain women made flowers from crêpe paper and thought them beautiful.

Molly and Kate stepped carefully between the mounds. They felt subdued and sad. Both were thinking of the lonely dead on this forlorn hillside.

"Here it is!" Molly called suddenly.

"Here what is?" Kate asked, hurrying to see.

"Little Johnny Corn's grave," Molly told her. "I was looking for it. It's exactly like his ma said when she told me about it."

She knelt on the ground to read the words carved on the tip-tilted stone. They said:

Little Johnny has left us now;
He's sleeping beneath the sod.
He's playing his harp
And dangling his little feet
Around the throne of God.

"Oh, Kate! Isn't it lovely?" Molly felt tears in her eyes. She wasn't a bit ashamed for Kate to see them either. How many years had little Johnny been buried here? There was no date. For all those years his mother had been paying ten cents a week to pay for her little boy's gravestone. How she must have loved him.

"Who would have thought old Mrs. Corn could write a poem?" Molly asked. She blinked away her tears.

Kate had been unusually quiet. Now she found her voice: "Stupid! She didn't write it. Mrs. Corn can't even sign her own name. My daddy says when she goes to vote, she has to make a cross mark where her name ought to go."

"Well, I think it's sweet just the same, whoever wrote it," Molly said. Again she felt tears behind her eyes. "I'm going to come back someday and bring flowers for Johnny's grave. Real flowers from Daddy's garden. Real zinnias, and some honeysuckle to smell sweet. Not ugly paper roses like these."

Kate had climbed ahead, to the top of the cemetery hill. There she waved urgently to Molly. Then she dropped flat to the ground in the tall grass. Molly hurried to catch up. Kate gave her a sign to lie down, too. She put a finger to her lips.

"Look!" she whispered when Molly caught up with her.

In the valley over the top of this hill, the girls saw a cluster of cabins, with a few outhouses. There were people, too, five or six of them. From here they looked like mice playing a game of Hide-and-Seek. Two men seemed to be chasing the others. They dashed first behind one cabin, then crouched behind another. It was like watching a movie on a tiny screen.

"What on earth are they doing?" Molly whispered into Kate's ear.

Just then there was a sharp *bang!* like a firecracker on the Fourth of July. Only it wasn't the Fourth of July. All but one of the men disappeared like a wink into the cabins. The doors closed. The one man left alone fell to the ground. There he lay still, like a forgotten doll.

Molly looked at Kate, whose face was as white as paper.

"Do you think—?" she whispered hoarsely.

"Yes, I do think they're bootleggers," Kate whispered back. "Come on. Let's go!"

The girls slithered on their stomachs over the rough ground, through the tall grass. Once out of sight of the cabins, they flew down the cemetery hill to Old England Road. It seemed like an old friend that would guide them home, if they hurried.

Stopping often to look behind, they ran until their sides hurt. There were no more shots. They met only one creaking wagon pulled by a team of oxen. Its driver was the peddler who sometimes sold kindling wood to Camp people. Though he looked straight ahead and did not speak, today he too seemed a friend. He might even protect them if they were in trouble with the bootleggers or maybe the sheriff.

At last the girls were back at Little Potato Creek. Crossing it this time, Molly slipped and got one shoe wet. It was one of her best oxfords, but who could care about such a trifle now?

The back gate squeaked when the girls banged it behind them.

"Lunchtime!" Vashti called through the kitchen window. Molly could see her yellow head rag shining. It was almost like a halo, she thought. Good old Vashti. "Tomato bisque and fresh brownies," she called to the girls. Was it really only lunchtime? Surely they had been gone for hours and hours.

"Where shall we say we've been?" Molly asked.

"Why, we've been playing games in gullies," Kate told her calmly. "We needn't say where those gullies were."

"Shall we tell about the gunshot and the bootleggers?"

Kate thought a minute.

"Maybe we'd better leave that to the sheriff," she decided. "We've seen things nobody else in Isabella even guesses about, even grown-ups."

Then she did something that wasn't like Kate. She put her arms around Molly and gave her a quick hug.

"Now we've got a real secret. Only friends have secrets. Good-bye!" she called, as she slammed the squeaky gate behind her and ran home for her own lunch.

4

PIANO RECITAL

The bath water was warm and fragrant with Mother's best violet-scented oil. Molly lay in the tub, examining her soapy hands. Since she had last noticed them, her fingers seemed to have grown longer. A lot depended upon those ten fingers at tonight's piano recital.

What if they forget that cadenza in "Romance"? she panicked suddenly. The cadenza was a fountain of soft notes, like a swallow dipping and swooping.

"If you strike a snag or have a lapse of memory," Miss Julie had said yesterday, "think of how the notes look on the page of music. Then your fingers will remember."

So Molly tried now to see the notes in her mind's eye. Yes, they were there, as plain as day.

"Hurry up!" Ruthie began to pound on the bathroom

door. "It's my turn in the tub. We have to leave at seven o'clock."

Molly dried herself fast. She fluffed Mother's best bath powder in a flowery cloud all over her. She pulled on her silk step-ins with lace, her camisole with blue ribbons around its top, her Sunday petticoat, and her white silk knee socks. Wearing best clothes, even underclothes, made her feel different and special.

Then there was a great flurry. Vashti helped the girls finish dressing. She tied the sash around Molly's rose voile dress. Its skirt was three tiers of soft ruffles. She tied green ribbon streamers on the shoulders of Ruth's dress. She rubbed a little Vaseline on their slippers to make them shine and put the silver barrette in Molly's hair. Daddy had bought it for her in Atlanta.

Penny hopped around the room; first on one foot,

then the other. Vashti had dressed her first, in her pink party dress, for she was going to the recital, too.

Mother had said, "Suppose Penny talks out loud and makes you forget your pieces?" But Penny wasn't a baby anymore. She promised to be good. "Good" meant quiet.

"If you remember, I'll let you play with Rebecca tomorrow," Molly told her. Rebecca was her own oldest and most beautiful bisque doll. She had long sat like a doll princess on the top toy shelf of the nursery, no longer played with and out of a little sister's threatening reach.

"You look sweet, all of you," Mother approved when she inspected the three girls. She herself looked lovely. Theirs was the prettiest of Isabella mothers, Molly thought for the hundredth time. She was wearing her dark blue satin dress with shining bugle beads and fringe around its hem. The fringe swished when she moved.

"My four girls," Daddy said, smiling. He set Penny in the crook of one arm. He kissed Mother and patted Ruth and Molly on their heads. "If you play your pieces to match the way you look, I'll be proud of you. Think of all those piano lessons I've paid for—years and years of them. All those hours of practising I've had to listen to, besides. I bet I could play that 'Romance' and Ruthie's 'Will-o'-the-Wisp' myself by this time."

Molly and Ruth looked at each other and stifled giggles. They'd like to hear him try. The best Daddy could do was play "Chopsticks" to tease them.

Once there, they found Miss Julie's living room arranged like a theater. Folding chairs from the clubhouse were set in rows. The baby grand piano stood in front of a bay window. All ten of her pupils sat in the front row. The youngest children, like Peter Collins and Susan Frye, were at one end; Kate and Molly at the other. It was grown-up and grand to be the oldest ones, now that Kate's sister Josie had graduated from Isabella School.

Molly looked sideways at Kate. She was wearing Josie's last year's recital dress. Something wasn't quite right about the color. Perhaps it had faded in the wash. It was now an ugly greenish yellow. It didn't go well with Kate's hair, which was carrot-colored (though Kate called it "auburn"). When she stood, the dress was too long, way below her knees. It made her look like a girl playing grown-up in someone else's clothes.

Molly felt sorry for Kate. Not everybody had mothers who could sew or even fit a dress for their daughters. She and Ruthie were lucky. For a minute she forgot Kate's "Mexican Hat Dance." She forgot that it was going to be more exciting to listen to than "Romance," which sounded easier than it was.

She smiled at Kate and squeezed her hand. It surprised Molly by being cold and clammy.

"You're not scared, are you?" she whispered.

"Not the teeniest bit!" Kate tossed her head and grinned. She was a little paler than usual, which made her freckles show more.

Then it was time for Miss Julie's speech of welcome to the parents. She looked dignified and grand in her long purple recital gown with its little train. She was wearing a jet necklace and silver bracelets. Now she took little Peter Collins's hand and led him to the piano.

He was just six and had had only a few music lessons. His chubby legs dangled from the piano bench. Molly thought of old Mrs. Corn's Johnny, who was dangling his feet this minute around the throne of God. Perhaps Johnny Corn had looked like Peter.

He played "Frère Jacques," one finger at a time, slowly and carefully, without a single mistake. When people clapped, he ran to his mother and hid his face in her skirt.

Next came Robin Cutler, who was seven. She played the melody from Papa Haydn's *Surprise Symphony*. Its surprise was a crashing chord at the end, meant to wake listeners who might have nodded. Robin had to stretch her fingers to reach the chord. Molly remembered playing that piece, long ago, when she was little.

Two more children took their turns. Only one, poor Susan Frye, forgot her piece right in its middle. No one breathed in an awful silence, for what seemed a long time. Only a moth bumped and bumped against a windowpane behind the piano. Susan fumbled and began again—three times. At last she remembered what came next. Then she sailed with a flourish through the maze of notes to the end of her piece.

Now it was Ruth's turn. Her skirts switched and her hair shone like spun gold as she half skipped to the piano.

"That's my sister!" a little voice piped suddenly. It was Penny. Before anyone could stop her, she slipped from Daddy's lap and ran to the piano. There she climbed onto the bench beside the astonished Ruth and folded her hands.

"Go on! Play!" she commanded her sister. Miss Julie

nodded. So, just as if nothing had happened, Ruth began "Will-o'-the-Wisp."

Never having seen one, Molly wasn't sure about will-o'-the-wisps. To her, Ruth's flying fingers always sounded like butterflies, if butterflies could make music. They flitted over the keys. Molly's heart puffed with pride in her middle sister.

Pride in two sisters, when it came to that. For Penny sat as still as a pink doll with yellow curls on the piano bench beside Ruth. When the piece ended, the two slid off the bench together. Ruth gave a dip of a curtsy, which Penny tried to copy and stumbled only a little. Did she think people were clapping for her?

"Don't you worry," Daddy whispered to Molly, as he picked up Penny and set her firmly back on his lap. "I won't let her get away when it's your turn to perform."

One by one Miss Julie's pupils played their pieces. Molly stole a glance at Mr. Turner now and then. At every recital for years he had quietly fallen asleep before it was half over. Suppose he should snore? The Turner family would be embarrassed. Tonight Molly was glad to see that he looked wide awake. Maybe Penny's little surprise act had amused him.

Then it was Molly's turn. Suddenly the piano looked a mile away. The air swirled in dizzy waves. Her hands were sticky. But Miss Julie was nodding at her, so Molly stood. She pulled up her left sock (that weak garter again!). Then without knowing how she got there, she was at the piano. Quite by themselves, her fingers began to play.

They played "Romance." It was a love song, like a serenade. She thought of a garden, silver in moonlight.

Two shadowy lovers were singing by a fountain. The notes were water drops.

Someday I'll write a poem about them, Molly thought. Her fingers flew lightly over the keys. Even the cadenza went as smoothly as the flight of a night bird through the dim garden.

Then it was over. For a minute no one applauded. Molly shook away her dream. She curtsied politely. As people began to clap, she stole a look at Daddy. He was clapping louder than anyone else. He grinned and winked at her. Oddly, Mother didn't smile at all. In fact her mouth was set in a thin line. Did she disapprove of something? It wasn't like Mother, whose hands lay still in her lap.

Did I do something wrong? Molly thought anxiously. But Miss Julie was smiling, so she felt better.

Kate didn't even look at her as Molly sat down. Molly understood. The room had begun to swim for Kate, too, for her turn was next. She almost ran to the piano. Tossing back her hair and sliding the bench a little closer, she began to play the "Mexican Hat Dance."

No question about it, Kate could really play. Yes, her best friend and rival had what Miss Julie called a "musical gift." Kate's fingers raced faster and faster through the leaping notes of her piece. Molly had seen pictures of Mexican dancers. They tossed their straw hats to the floor and danced wildly round and round the wide brims. Faster and faster went Kate's fingers now. She was inspired. At last the music ended with a crashing chord. The audience clapped wildly, to match.

"You were wonderful!" Molly told Kate. To her own surprise, she meant it.

The recital was over for another year. Everyone breathed freely again. Mothers were no longer tense and fearful that their children would forget their pieces in the middle. Fathers stood tall and proud. They clapped each other on the back and congratulated the young musicians. Mothers kissed their sons and daughters. Little boys dashed in and out among the grown-ups. They drank cup after cup of Miss Julie's pineapple punch from the refreshment table. They hid extra cookies in their pockets.

Miss Julie leaned to whisper into Molly's ear.

"I knew 'Romance' was the right piece for my girl with the sensitive touch," she said softly. "Your fingers wove a magic garden with a pair of lovers singing in the moonlight."

Molly felt her eyes grow wide with wonder. Was it true that music could speak the same language to two hearts? She had suspected it to be true, but had never been sure. Here was a thought to dream upon. But why, she still wondered, had Mother looked severe and disapproving?

On the way home, Molly asked her.

Mother was astonished. "Why, dear, I was trying so hard not to look too proud," she said. "I didn't mean to look disapproving. How could I be that, with two daughters who played their pieces so prettily?"

Yes, Recital Day was over. Now Molly lay in a streak of moonlight that fell across her bed. She was still too excited to sleep. Bits of "Romance" floated like broken clouds through her thoughts. She could still hear the lover serenading his lady in a moonlit garden.

I didn't need to see the notes in my mind's eye, she

thought. My fingers remembered all those notes without my reminding them at all. Molly held up her hands in the dim light from the window.

Then, sleepily, she began to wonder what there now was to look forward to. Days after red-letter days were often dull. Then Molly smiled to herself in the dark.

I'd almost forgotten, she thought. Next week Cousin Eva is coming. She's my favorite grown-up and a Lady Poet.

5

ON KIMSEY
MOUNTAIN

"*Must* we drive all the way to the top of that mountain?" Cousin Eva asked Daddy. "I'm perfectly happy just seeing it from here." She stared anxiously at the narrow clay road just ahead. It wound its way higher and higher, like a thin string, to the crest of Kimsey Mountain. She gripped the handle of the Studebaker's front door tightly.

"Of course we must go up," Daddy replied cheerfully. "You have to see the view from the top. You can see the whole Copper Basin from there. It really looks like its name, you know—a copper-colored bowl with a green mountain rim. It's a sight you won't forget."

"You mustn't worry." Mother leaned from the back seat as the car began to climb. She put her hand on Cousin Eva's shoulder. "William is a fine driver. There's never been an accident on our Kimsey Highway. On the

way up, everyone hugs the bank; on the way down, everyone honks on curves. That warns other drivers."

"Our chestnuts grow on the other side of the mountain," Ruth piped up. "We go to Dead Man's Gap every October for chestnuts and a picnic. Like today."

"I love picnics," Penny said. She bounced up and down on the jump seat of the car. The fat picnic basket was stuffed under it. The freezer of lemon sherbet was on Ruth's side. With Mother in the middle, beside her, there was little room for Molly's legs. She didn't mind. For perfect ages she had looked forward to Cousin Eva's first trip up the mountain.

When she returned to her own home, Cousin Eva was going to write a book of poems about mountains. Every day she made notes on a little pad with a silk cover. Before coming to Tennessee, she had written Mother, "My next poems will be about the mountains that you will show me. 'I will lift mine eyes unto the hills,' like the Psalmist, and be inspired."

Her first book was named *River Acres*. Its poems were hard to understand, and they had no rhymes at all. They were about the eastern Carolinas. They spoke of marshes choked with hyacinths, slow rivers, fields of cotton and tobacco, wide flatlands under a pale sky. There was a lot also about the dark workers in those fields who stripped tobacco leaves and picked cotton under a hot sun.

What beautiful poems she would now write about hills and mountains, Molly thought. About hill people and their stiff, silent pride. About how they dug bright copper from deep underground. Kate would be impressed (so would be everyone in Isabella) when she read Cousin Eva's mountain poems. Nobody else had a poet for a cousin.

Still, from the first day of her visit, something had seemed wrong. When Cousin Eva had stepped from the train at Copperhill Station, there were cinders on her hat brim and a smudge on her nose. Her white gloves looked gray. Her hair hung in damp wisps instead of curls around her lovely face. Of course, everyone expected the one-a-day train from Asheville to be dirty. But Cousin Eva liked to look, Daddy often said, as if she had "just stepped from a bandbox."

She clung to Mother for a long minute. She was trembling.

"Mary!" she wailed. "The trip was awful—like being on a roller coaster. I was scared within an inch of my life. Why, in one place the track was too steep for the train to reach the top. It had to back up and try again!"

Molly and Ruth looked at each other and swallowed giggles. The train often had that trouble. Everyone laughed about the Copper Basin's "Little Engine That Could."

By now Cousin Eva had been in Isabella for a week. She and Mother talked for hours every day, about being girls together long ago. Daddy showed her his prize chrysanthemums, his pansy bed, and the rabbits. She listened to Ruth and Molly play their recital pieces and was sure both girls were "gifted." She told Penny enchanting bedtime stories every night. She loved Vashti's ice box rolls and Mother's orange angel cake. Ladies of Isabella Camp had called and met the lady poet from beyond the mountains. Parties were being planned. The visit was going well.

Today was a high point. It was "gypsy weather," Molly thought. The first October frost had splashed sourwood, maple, and sycamore trees with red, gold, and russet. The mountain air was crisp and cool. Cool enough for knicker suits to feel good. Molly hated hers with a purple passion, but Mother insisted on knickers for walking in the woods. Knickers and a long-sleeved middy blouse discouraged briar scratches and chiggers.

Now the car climbed slowly, for the road was steep. Past Hairpin Bend, where they had often picnicked. Past Cold Springs. There, lilies of the valley bloomed in a fragrant carpet under the trees in May. Past the bank where arbutus half hid under forest mold in March and where they later picked blueberries in July. Past the bare red gash where a landslide had stripped the forest away after a torrent of rain.

Because trees on this side of Kimsey Mountain were

young and low-growing, the view was open. Molly tried to keep her eyes on the far distance. To look straight down from the edge of the road made her dizzy—not really mountain-sick, but dizzy.

"This must be the way it feels to be in an airplane," she leaned forward to tell Cousin Eva. "We can see the whole world from here almost."

Cousin Eva said nothing, which seemed a little strange. Usually, being a poet, she described things in a flowery way.

There was Isabella, far below. Copperhill and Ducktown, too. The three mining camps looked like toy villages. Just beyond were the copper furnaces. From here, their chimneys were like cigarettes, standing on end. All were blowing yellow, white, and orange smoke clouds into the air. Cigarettes for my giant, Molly daydreamed.

They climbed and climbed. From the set of his head, anybody who knew him could tell that Daddy was happy. He was proud of his Studebaker touring car, the daring Kimsey Highway, and his expert driving. If Cousin Eva would only show more interest, rave a little, Daddy would be so pleased.

Suddenly, like a jack rabbit from a hole, a car came round the next bend. No one had seen or heard its coming. Daddy turned quickly into the bank. Cousin Eva jerked open the car door and jumped onto the running board. She also screamed.

Mother leaned over to grab her coat and pull her back. Daddy jammed on the brakes. He stopped the car with a jerk. Cousin Eva was sobbing now; so was Penny.

"There was really no danger, dear," Mother said calmly. "I have perfect confidence in William's driving. He's quite used to mountain roads."

Cousin Eva stopped shaking and tried to smile.

"I'm sorry," she apologized. "I've just never seen the world from the sky like this. Everything looks different and dangerous. Do go on, William. I'll try not to look down for a while."

"Keep your hand off the door handle, please," Daddy said a little crossly. "It makes me nervous, thinking you might jump out and be hurt."

Everyone was quiet as mice the rest of the way to the top of Kimsey Mountain. There everyone got out to stretch and look. Though Molly thought her pale, Cousin Eva tried to admire the view.

"Well, I declare!" Daddy said suddenly. His eyes were shining like a boy's. "Look at that persimmon tree! We've beat the possums and the raccoons for once. That tree is loaded with ripe fruit."

In a trice he was halfway up its trunk, shaking the branches. Wrinkled orange persimmons, bigger than cherries, showered to the ground. The girls squealed with delight.

"Taste one," Mother told Cousin Eva. "There was a frost last night, so they'll be sweet as honey."

Molly and Ruth laughed. They remembered tasting unripe persimmons once. To tease them, Daddy had offered them two bright orange ones with smooth skins. How their mouths had puckered and eyes watered after the first bite! Never again would they taste a "green" persimmon. Today, after a nip of frost, the fruit was wrinkled and ugly, but tasted like sweet plums.

"Just wait 'til you taste Mary's persimmon pudding," Daddy told Cousin Eva. By now the girls had filled his old plaid driving cap and a coffee can. "It's like ambrosia of the gods," he bragged, licking his lips at the thought.

Mother looked pleased. "It's really more like sweet potato pudding," she said modestly, "if you happen to like that."

Back in the car, spirits rose.

"We're almost there, at our chestnut grove," Ruthie said. No one mentioned Dead Man's Gap. The name might upset Cousin Eva again. Molly remembered its story. Mountain people said a lone hunter had frozen to death in the gap, long years ago. His broken tombstone was still there. Nearby was a second marker. This belonged, folks told, to a woman who had burned to death in a campfire on the spot. Molly shivered. Dead Man's Gap was a lonely place even on this bright day.

It was a good year for chestnuts. They lay thick on the ground beneath the giant trees. Once out of the car, Cousin Eva was brisk and eager. Imagine! She had never before seen a chestnut tree. Nor had she known that three satiny brown nuts grow in each burr. The round, prickly green burrs were like little porcupines.

Now the first frost had burst open those burrs. It had killed chiggers, too, Molly thought. Goody! That meant no salt water bath tonight to keep chigger bites from making skins itchy and miserable tomorrow.

Daddy took the bushel basket from the trunk of the car. Each girl pulled on a pair of thick gloves. Chestnut burrs were as sharp as porcupine quills. The girls wouldn't have minded a few prickles today; not with the prospect of roasted chestnuts all next winter. Even raw, the nuts were sweet to nibble, though too many might bring on a stomachache, Mother warned.

By the time the girls had filled the basket, the two ladies had spread their picnic on a flat rock. Penny was already waving a leg of fried chicken. No one needed calling twice.

"This air makes me hungry." Cousin Eva bit into an olive. She looked pink and pretty again. No one told her that she was losing a hairpin from a side curl. "This is my first mountain picnic, and I'm starved!"

So was everyone. Fried chicken and potato salad. Lettuce sandwiches and deviled eggs. Hot coffee from one thermos bottle and hot soup from another.

It's really too cool for sherbet in October," Mother said, as she opened the freezer. No one agreed with her. Sherbet and fudge cake disappeared in a trice.

Shadows grew longer and the air cooler, almost cold. Molly shivered and tried not to look at the two forlorn tombstones. The family piled quickly into the car. Suddenly it seemed like a piece of home.

"I think I'd like to ride in the back seat this time," Cousin Eva said firmly. "I'll sit on the bank side and try not to look down. I might even shut my eyes on Hairpin Bend."

It seemed a good idea. Even then, she looked frightened. On the way down the mountain, no one felt like talking. Penny curled in Mother's lap. Everybody thought she was asleep.

Daddy drove very carefully. He was now on the outside of the road. This was more dangerous, everyone knew. The car seemed to swing and sway from side to side. Down and down, curve after curve.

Penny was *not* asleep. In a little while she began to look a little gray, almost green.

"You'd better stop, William," Mother said quietly. It was too late. Before Penny could be lifted out to the roadside, she was sick. Chicken and fudge cake came up in a swoop. Poor little girl! Poor everybody, really. For it happened twice more. The smell and the motion of the car made everyone queasy.

Finally Daddy said, "Sorry, but I can't stop again, no matter what. See that fog bank farther down? We don't want to be caught in that. It's rising fast. The Thompsons had to spend the night in their car on Kimsey Mountain once. In a pea-soup fog just like that."

Even Mother looked worried now. Cousin Eva's eyes had a wild look. Molly tried to imagine spending a night on the mountain. Hill people told stories about bears and wildcats. She also knew about landslides.

"I'm sick, too!" Ruthie wailed suddenly.

Daddy didn't stop the car this time. Instead, he reached into the glove drawer and pulled out several brown paper bags.

"Here," he said grimly. "Use these."

It was a miserable ride home. Poor Penny and Ruth used up two bags each. Even Molly, who was proud of never being carsick, felt queasy in her stomach. She swallowed hard and tried to think of something nice, like swimming in cool water.

Mother held the heads of the two girls to comfort them. She herself looked frazzled. Cousin Eva's head rolled from side to side. Her eyes were tight-shut. She was as white as the paper wings of a moth. What if she too were really carsick? A lady poet, Molly felt sure, would never stop being embarrassed.

Daddy drove slowly now—round and round the curves; down, down, down. The car struck the fog bank just before it reached the foot of the mountain. The fog was like gray milk.

"Oh, do be careful!" Mother warned. Her voice quivered.

What do you think I'm being?" Daddy snapped. It was not like him to snap. "It might help if you'd walk a little ahead, Mary, and hold the flashlight."

So Mother (poor Mother who was timid about the dark) did this. The extra light didn't do much good. But suddenly the car burst out of the fog. Down here, at the foot of the mountain, the moon was shining! And the orange glow from the copper furnaces was like a beacon light, for tired travelers.

Once there, home had never been more warm and welcoming. Everybody cheered up enough to thank Daddy for being such a good driver.

"You're our hero, Daddy," Ruthie told him, giving him a loud kiss.

Thank you for saving our lives, Molly thought, though she didn't say it out loud. Mother and Cousin Eva hugged each other without a word.

Vashti had gone to bed long ago. Mother brewed a pot of strong tea. Even Ruth and Penny were allowed some, with lots of sugar and milk.

"Tea is the best thing for settling stomachs," Mother said firmly. Cousin Eva drank three cups—boiling hot, with no milk and sugar.

Her bed was like a cloud pillow, Molly thought before she fell asleep. For a minute or two it seemed to sway a little, like the car weaving its way down the mountain. It had been a day to remember, both happy and miserable. She wondered drowsily just how much of it she would tell Kate. She couldn't bear it if Kate, or anybody else, laughed at Cousin Eva's fear of mountains. The day had been a mixed adventure that turned out, like a fairy story, happily. Maybe Cousin Eva would forget the frightening part.

Except that she'll probably never write a poem about Kimsey Mountain, Molly thought as she dropped off to sleep. What a shame! For who except Cousin Eva could ever turn Molly's favorite mountain into poetry—even without rhyme?

6

DOWN ISABELLA MINE

Next day at lunchtime, Daddy turned to Cousin Eva.

"Well," he said, passing her a plate of buttermilk biscuits. "We gave you a bit of excitement yesterday, didn't we?"

Cousin Eva smiled faintly. "I had no idea this was such wild and woolly country," she replied. "I'm not a brave woman."

"Brave enough, I'm sure," Daddy said, "to take that trip I promised you, down a mine. You'll be the first woman to go underground into the Isabella shaft. I had the devil of a time getting the mine captain's permission. Until I told him you're a lady with real pluck."

Molly almost swallowed an olive pit. What wouldn't she give to go along? She knew better than to ask. No child, even one almost twelve, would ever be allowed down Isabella Mine. Would even a grown woman like Cousin Eva dare to go?

She needn't have wondered. Cousin Eva *was* plucky. She swallowed hard. The hand holding her butter knife quivered. Still, she looked Daddy firmly in the eye and said, "Yes, William, I will go down. If I am to write poems about mountains, I must also write about the underworld. What time tomorrow? And what does one wear on a trip down a mine shaft?"

"Any old thing," Daddy told her. "Jim, the mine captain, will dress you."

Mother gave Daddy a black look. Cousin Eva choked on a crumb and excused herself from the table. When she returned, she ate very little floating island, which was her favorite dessert.

"Tomorrow is Saturday. May Kate and I watch you go down in the lift?" Molly asked.

At that Mother burst out, "Oh, William, do you think it wise for two girls to hang around the mine entrance like that?"

Daddy considered, then said, "I don't see what harm it could do. They can watch us go down, then wait in Jim's office until we come up. It will be a good experience."

Molly rushed to the phone to tell Kate.

In the mine captain's office next morning, the two girls watched as Cousin Eva was dressed for the mine. She was shocked when she saw the dirty coverall offered her. Her arms and feet were lost in it. Captain Jim turned up the legs and cuffs, over and over. He put huge boots on her dainty feet. She could hardly take a step in them. Then came enormous gloves, stiff with

dirt. He set a miner's cap on her head. It hid her soft brown curls.

"I've never seen you look prettier," Daddy teased Cousin Eva. She made a wry face.

"Whatever you do, don't take my picture," she told him. "And don't show me a mirror either. I couldn't stand the shock."

Daddy dressed himself in miners' clothes. Captain Jim lighted the flames in the lanterns on their caps.

"It'll be dark where we're going," he explained. "There's nothing to worry about, though. There's no danger down below. We're not blasting this month."

Molly and Kate looked at each other. They knew about blasting, but Cousin Eva didn't. When a new tunnel was opened up with dynamite in the mine, all of Isabella Camp shook. It was like a little earthquake. Once a crystal goblet in Mother's china cabinet had shattered. No, they hadn't thought about blasting.

It was time. Daddy, Captain Jim, and Cousin Eva walked stiffly in their miners' clothes to the shaft of Isabella Mine. They stepped onto the lift. It was not at all, Molly thought, like elevators she'd ridden in Atlanta. Instead, the mine lift was a square of wooden planks with a thick cable on each corner. There were no sides or railings to hold on to.

"We'll be back up in half an hour," Daddy called, as the cables began to turn on their great wheels. Cousin Eva said nothing at all. She neither smiled nor waved as the lift disappeared slowly down the mine shaft.

They look like trolls, Molly thought. She shivered. The little lamps on their caps shone so feebly. It would be dark as pitch where they were going.

"I'd be scared to go underground," Kate admitted. To Molly's surprise, she added, "I think your cousin is brave to do it."

The girls returned to the shack that was Captain Jim's office. There they sat down to wait. Time passed at a snail's pace. Molly doodled on a scrap of paper. Kate rocked in Captain Jim's swivel chair. It squeaked like a frightened mouse.

"You know why miners don't want women underground, don't you?" Kate asked.

"No." Molly had never heard this.

"It's because miners are superstitious. They think a woman down a mine means bad luck. She might cast an evil spell. Then somebody would be killed by falling rock."

Molly shivered. What a horrible thing to tell her

now! She couldn't help wondering: Was there a grain of truth in the miners' superstition? Were those four thick cables on the lift really strong enough not to break? The hands of the clock on Captain Jim's desk didn't seem to move at all. What was happening right this minute to the three trolls underground?

Molly looked at her doodling. Such ugly designs she had been making! They were all ink blots and blurs. Usually, while thinking of something else, she drew birds and daisies.

"I guess I'm glad they wouldn't let us go down," she admitted. Telling Kate helped a little.

Just then they heard a hoarse *squeak, squeak.* It was the cables. The lift was coming up. Both girls raced outside. But, instead of the three trolls, the lift held carts of mineral ore. It looked like ordinary rock, broken into chunks. As they watched, the ore was dumped into a boxcar waiting on a nearby track.

"Is that copper?" Kate asked, astonished. "I always thought copper was a shining color, like the sun."

"Ore from Isabella Mine has lots of copper *in* it," Molly told her. Where had Kate been all her life not to know that? "Ore has to be melted in a furnace. They call that 'smelting.' I guess smelting separates copper from iron and zinc and just plain rock."

The lift went down. After a long wait, it began rising again from the deep mine shaft. This time it held their trolls. Slowly, up from darkness into daylight, came three miners' caps, then human figures. Two were tall. Though Molly and Kate would never have recognized her, the little one must be Cousin Eva. Her face was smeared with dirt. Once Molly had seen a deer leap across a forest path. Cousin Eva's eyes had the deer's same frightened look.

But they were safe! Molly dashed to welcome her two trolls back to the bright world of air and sunlight.

"Don't kiss me yet." Cousin Eva held her away. She turned to Captain Jim and managed a small smile through the dirt. Then, "Oh, William!" she cried. "Please take me home. I want a hot bath more than anything else in all the world."

"We'll do that," Daddy promised her. "First we'll take off our miners' clothes. Then, while we're here, we'll look at the smelter. That's what we call the copper furnaces. If the girls go with us, they'll learn something, too."

At the smelter they watched from a safe distance. Ore from boxcars was poured into a giant furnace. Great fires roared beneath it. The furnace was like a monster without a name, Molly thought. Like a witch's cauldron or a dragon with a fiery mouth. Even from here their faces burned. How could Cousin Eva be shivering in such heat?

"Now watch!" Daddy told them. A hole opened on one side of the furnace. Molten copper began to pour from it into iron molds on a moving track below. It was beautiful, like liquid gold.

"When it cools," Daddy added, "we'll have chunks of almost pure copper. What's left we'll sell as other minerals and chemicals. Nothing will be wasted!"

Back at home, Mother met them at the gate. She took one look, then threw her arms around Cousin Eva, dirt and all.

"You should never have taken her down into that

mine, William," she scolded Daddy. "Poor dear. Just look at her."

"I learned a lot," Cousin Eva said weakly. "I feel ten years older and wiser."

So did Molly, though she hadn't been down in the shaft. And how proud she was. Her poet cousin was the first woman ever to dare the dark underworld of Isabella Mine. Kate, she noticed, mumbled a "thank you," gave Cousin Eva a respectful look, and went home.

That night the family toasted chestnuts around the fire. Molly still felt she had been in a faraway land, though really only a mile away from this cozy hearth.

Cousin Eva had been quiet all through dinner.

"What was it really like underground?" Molly asked her now.

"Have you ever heard of Hades?" her cousin replied. "It's the dark and gloomy Underworld. Ancient people believed it was the home of dead souls. That's what it was like underground."

"Oh, Eva!" Daddy was shocked. "Surely it wasn't that bad!"

"Maybe not quite. But those tunnels were so cold and black and wet. Their rough walls looked like any other ugly rock. I had expected to see bright copper shining through the darkness. And the noises!" Cousin Eva shuddered. "There was the awful rumble of the ore carts, besides the hacking of the picks of those poor miners. It all but made me deaf."

"They're not poor." Daddy sounded hurt. "They're very well paid."

"The canaries aren't paid, I'm sure," she retorted.

"Poor caged birds. Think of God's winged creatures never seeing sunshine and never flying freely! No wonder they don't sing."

"What canaries?" Ruthie asked, fishing a hot chestnut from the firecoals. Mother looked surprised.

"Those canaries are there to save men's lives," Daddy said stiffly. "If a bird droops, it means the air is not good. The miners escape safely, with no harm done. There's something you don't understand, Eva. If men want pennies or copper wire for electricity, or a hundred other useful things, there must be copper mines. Mary was right, I guess. I should never have taken you down into Isabella Mine."

Cousin Eva bit her lip and said nothing.

"Now, William," Mother spoke quickly in her let's-change-the-subject voice. "That's enough about mines. There are other things to think about. Things like our party for Eva next Saturday night. I've made the list. We'll have eight tables of bridge. And I've promised the guests that our lady cousin will give a poetry reading from her book."

Cousin Eva brightened. She took a hot chestnut Molly had peeled for her and tasted its sweet kernel.

"Oh, Mary, what shall I wear for the party?" she asked. She sounded like herself again. "I've been saving my sapphire gown with sequins for a special occasion."

"This is it," Mother said. The two ladies smiled at each other, Molly thought, like two girls with a secret.

7

COUSIN EVA'S PARTY

Cousin Eva's party was tonight, so the whole house was a beehive.

"I'm gonna polish this here piano 'til you kin see your face in it," Vashti said. She rubbed and rubbed. Her dark face shone with perspiration. Mrs. Corn was scrubbing the front porch on her hands and knees. A forest of little tables filled the front rooms. Ruth was setting out cards and ashtrays. Penny wasn't helping. Instead, she was playing house under one of the bridge tables with Puff, a family of dolls, and her Dutch tea set.

"Take that there cat out of here, Penny," Vashti told her. "I doesn't want it to jump on this pianer and scratch it. You know Puff don't belong in the house nohow. It's a outdoor cat."

Penny crawled from her card-table house. She picked

up Puff by the middle and put her kitty out the front door. Mother didn't allow cats in the house anyway.

In the kitchen, Mother's face was rosy from the stove's heat. She pulled another batch of meringues from the oven.

"I'm about to turn into a meringue!" she said. "This makes thirty-six. Don't you think that ought to be enough? One big meringue on each plate, with ice cream and mint-chocolate sauce?"

Molly set the last purple pansy in the Wedgwood bowl. She had done two bowls of pansies and three tall vases of Daddy's yellow chrysanthemums for the party.

"Will there be any meringues left over for us?" she asked. "We all love them."

Mother scraped the mixing bowl to make three more.

"These will be for you children," she said, "in case the others are all eaten tonight at the party. Now, dear, go see what Cousin Eva is doing. Perhaps she'd like to meet the train from Atlanta with your father." She brushed a wisp of damp hair from her face and looked worried. "Suppose the mints and nuts don't come from the confectioner. What on earth would we do?"

"Don't worry," Molly smoothed Mother's ruffled feathers. "If that happens, we'll think of something. Make our own candy maybe."

"Your flowers look lovely, dear." Mother gave Molly a quick kiss. Absentmindedly, she took out a pansy and cut the stems of three chrysanthemums. "Oh, I forgot to tell you. I asked Mr. Tyler to bring his flute this evening. When the card game is over, he will play Mozart's "Sonatina." Then Eva will read her poems. Won't that be lovely? Kate is coming to play the piano for her father. You'll like having your friend at the party, I'm sure. Now run along and speak to Cousin Eva."

Molly's heart missed a beat. The party lost its glow. Why did Kate have to come at all, much less play in front of everybody? Why hadn't Mother told her before the last minute like this? It was Cousin Eva's party, not Mr. Tyler's. He wasn't a good musician, anyway. Sometimes he didn't play his flute quite in tune.

She wondered what Daddy would think of adding music to the poetry reading after the bridge game. He hadn't liked the poetry idea at all. Molly had heard him tell Mother, "The men won't be happy to have to listen to poems, Mary. Most men don't care for that sort of thing."

"Well, it's about time they develop a little artistic taste," Mother had said, tossing her head. "Besides, who else in Isabella has a lady poet for a cousin? We must show her off. And Jim Tyler's music will add just the right touch." When Mother made up her mind, that was that.

Molly found Cousin Eva in her room. No, she didn't care to meet the Atlanta train with Daddy. On her face she wore a mask of cucumber and oatmeal cream. Her hair was wet. It hung down the back of her old Japanese kimono. She was practising for the poetry reading.

"A-E-I-O-U." She pronounced the vowels roundly and slowly, over and over. "These are my elocution exercises," she explained to Molly. "My voice must be clear and true tonight. Do remind me, if I forget, to suck a lemon dipped in sugar just before I read. Lemon is excellent for the voice. Now help me, dear. I'm trying to choose which of my poems to read."

She gave Molly a copy of *River Acres*. In it were stuck three ribbon bookmarks.

"Read these and tell me if you think they're my best."

The first poem began:

> The flatland sunsets glowing far and free,
> The flatland stillness of the stars,
> Where shadowy shapes of sunlight die, I go.

The words painted a picture that Molly could almost see. Another said:

> We walk through sunlit reeds by the river way
> Where gnarled oaks droop their old gray moss
> Above the water, mirroring
> Your beauty.

Molly could imagine the Lady of the Lake, walking beneath dripping southern moss.

The third poem was almost a little story:

> Look back to me, bright sun-browned boy
>   in the fields,
> Look back from your work, picking up
>   broken cornstalks
> From the dark earth as I pass by.
> A slim girl brings you water in a stone jug
> From a clear spring. She is beauty and music,
> And her step is proud.

"Oh, Cousin Eva, how can I possibly choose? You must read them all three." Cousin Eva began drying her damp hair.

I wonder if *my* hair will have golden lights in it someday, like hers, Molly thought. Right now her hair was plain brown, not even wavy.

"Now, didn't you tell me you have written some poetry, too?" her cousin asked. "Let me hear a sample now, while I comb my hair."

So Molly brought her own poem about fire on Angelico Mountain. She had watched the fire one night from her window when there was no moon. Molly's heart pounded now as she read, for her poems were secrets. She hadn't even told Mother about them. Certainly not Kate, who would laugh and toss her red hair and call her "Silly!" Molly was tired of being called silly.

Her voice quivered as she read. Perhaps she needed elocution lessons, like Cousin Eva's. She almost swallowed a word or two at first. The rest she read with as much expression as she could:

> Fire, fire on my mountain,
> Like a Chinese dragon
> Your hot breath burns the maples.
> Your hot tongue licks the pine trees.
> You are beautiful in the night, but I hate you,
> For you leave my mountain black and dead.

"I tried writing a poem that doesn't rhyme," Molly told Cousin Eva shyly. "It's easy to write free verse, isn't it?"

"Writing poetry is never easy," her cousin said. "You are my heart's own child. When I go home, you must send me all your poems. They will be our secret. Someday you will write a book of poetry like mine, only better."

Without meaning to do it, suddenly Molly told Cousin Eva her most secret secret.

"I've already sent my 'Fire' poem to *St. Nicholas* magazine," she said in a rush of words. "Every month it prints children's poems and stories, if the editor thinks they're good enough. Do you think he'll like mine?"

"I wouldn't be a bit surprised." Cousin Eva smiled. "When I go home, you must write me what happens."

"You won't tell anybody, will you?" Molly asked. "Not even Mother?"

Cousin Eva crossed her heart. So now they had a secret, she and her real-poet cousin.

After a supper of leftovers (the kind nobody likes), it was time to dress for the party. Penny was tucked into bed early with no story (she didn't like that ei-

ther). Ruth could stay up until nine o'clock and greet the guests. So both Molly and Ruth hurried into their rose and green recital dresses and tied each other's sashes.

The two girls dashed back and forth between the ladies' bedrooms. Mother's shoulders needed powdering. (Molly looked into the mirror at her own bony ones. Would they ever be smooth and beautiful like Mother's?) Cousin Eva's necklace needed clasping. All the hooks on Mother's camisole had to be fastened. It was hard to make them come out even at the top.

Then it was time for the curling iron. Molly and Ruth were not to be trusted with this. What if they scorched a curl? So the two ladies rolled each other's hair in soft ringlets around their faces.

Finally Cousin Eva slipped her evening gown over her head. It was the color of sapphires and shimmered with sequins. Mother's gown was ashes of roses. Its skirt fell in points to the floor. How lovely they both looked—like magazine cover pictures.

"I know!" Molly exclaimed. "Cousin Eva is the Bluebird of Happiness, and Mother is Queen of Roses." The two ladies laughed. They also looked pleased. They stole quick glances in the long mirror and patted their hair one last time.

"Here come the first guests!" Daddy called. It was Mr. Tyler and Kate, with the flute in its case and a roll of music. Kate looked like the cat that swallowed the canary, Molly thought. Why not? She was going to play the piano for everyone to hear and admire. While Molly sat in the corner and had to listen. Kate set the music on the piano rack. She was wearing the greenish yellow dress that had faded in the wash.

There was a flurry of other guests arriving, then finding their places at card tables. The bridge game began. The hubbub of voices settled into a hum.

For a while Molly and Kate sat on the sofa, watching the game. Ruth went to bed, after milk and cookies in the kitchen. Molly wondered if she would like to play bridge someday. Perhaps when she was old, maybe twenty. Grown-ups seemed to enjoy it. She listened to the drone of voices all around: "Are hearts trumps?" "I bid a little slam and made it!" "You villain! You trumped my ace! I'll never forgive you!"

Mrs. Frye made a mock face at Mr. Miller, who was her partner. None of it made much sense. The new game of Mah-Jongg was more fun than this silly bridge. Mother had promised Molly a Mah-Jongg party for her next birthday.

At ten o'clock she slipped into the kitchen to help Vashti set out dessert plates and coffee cups. Vashti had taken off her yellow head rag. She was wearing a ruffled maid's cap instead. They filled fluted nut cups and silver candy dishes. The pink and white mints were in shapes of rosebuds and lilies. They were terribly tempting. Molly tasted just one broken crumb when Vashti wasn't looking.

Then Mother came through the door. Her cheeks were pink, her eyes shining with excitement.

"Quick! I need a cut lemon for Miss Eva," she told Vashti. Then, "Come back with the guests, Molly. Mr. Tyler and Kate are about to play."

As if I wanted to hear them, Molly thought disagreeably. But she followed Mother and returned to the sofa. From here she could watch both Kate's face and fingers as she played. Mr. Tyler put the pieces of his flute together, tried a note or two, then nodded to Kate.

Molly had heard them play the "Sonatina" many times. It was their best piece. The music was lovely, she had to admit. Tonight Mr. Tyler played mostly in tune. Mr. Miller, who sat near the piano, winced only once or twice when there was a screechy note.

Kate's face was stiff. She was pale, though her freckles showed more than ever. Her fingers flew easily over the keys. Just once she stumbled over a trill. Probably no one noticed it.

I could have played just as well, Molly thought. That music is easy as pie. I wish Daddy played an instrument, instead of growing pansies and snapdragons.

Then she thought of how much everyone enjoyed Daddy's flowers. He had the only garden in Isabella. She thought of the fresh blossom he always wore in his buttonhole. She was a little ashamed of being jealous of Kate.

Why, that's what's the matter with me, she thought. I'm jealous!

"Jealous folks gets green eyes," Vashti had told her once. That, of course, was just Vashti making up a story. But if there was a grain of truth in it, Molly didn't want to risk green eyes.

"Molly's eyes are her best feature," Mother often said. "They're lovely hyacinth blue." Molly secretly agreed, though she would never have said so.

Now it was time for Cousin Eva to read her poetry.

"Isn't she beautiful?" Mrs. Tyler whispered behind her fan. Indeed her cousin was. Daddy, Molly noticed, looked uneasy. She remembered that he had not encouraged the poetry reading.

Molly looked at the other men. She had to admit they did not seem eager for what was coming. What if Cousin Eva's poems fell flat? What if no one liked them?

The lady poet stood now in the curve of the piano. She did indeed look like the Bluebird of Happiness. Cousin Eva's face shone. Her eyes seemed to gaze at some faraway beauty. She began to read about her flatlands; about trees with long gray moss, under which sad ladies wept; about sea birds flying low over salt marshes.

It was her voice that worried Molly. Not the vowels. They were as round and clear as half a lemon and all that elocution practise could make them. But Cousin Eva didn't sound like herself. Her voice was like that of a ghostly spirit, speaking from far away. Was that the way to read poetry? Molly and Kate stole a look at each other. Both were uncomfortable. Why didn't Cousin Eva read in her sweet, natural voice?

The guests seemed to wonder, too. Mr. Martin crossed and recrossed his long legs. Mr. Frye sucked loudly on his pipe, until his wife stepped on his toes under the table. Captain Jim cleared his throat loudly and began to shuffle a deck of cards. Daddy's face grew red, and Mother looked a little wild. No one had expected anything so embarrassing.

Only Cousin Eva was not at all disturbed. She was reading her poetry to people whose hearts, she was sure, were in tune with her spirit.

Suddenly there was a commotion in the library. A lady's voice gave a little shriek. Mother and Daddy dashed to see what was the matter. So did two of the men guests. Cousin Eva looked startled. She stopped reading in the middle of a word.

"It's the cat!" someone said. "Who let it in? Mrs. McFee is terrified of cats. She's a high-strung woman."

Just then, as if a wild dog were on her tail, Puff dashed from the library. In and out, under the card tables, she scurried through the tangle of legs. Her ears were flat. She was terrified. Molly jumped to open the front door, to help Puff escape. What on earth had their gentle cat done?

She beckoned to Kate. The two girls slipped quietly through the library door. There they found Mrs. McFee slumped in her chair. She was wild-eyed and as pale as paper. Daddy was holding a glass of something to her lips, while Mother fanned her vigorously. Mr. Collins rubbed her hands.

"I'm all right now," Mrs. McFee said weakly. She pulled herself together, sat up straight, and smiled faintly. "It's foolish of me, I know. But cats scare me within an inch of my life. One scratched me badly when I was a baby." She shuddered. "I've always been sure the dreadful creatures are instruments of the devil."

Molly and Kate tried not to giggle. Puff, an instrument of the devil? Why, she had never even caught a mouse.

Cousin Eva looked like a wilted lily. She slumped into the nearest chair. "Don't ask me to read anymore," she whispered to Mother, who was looking frantic. "That awful cat has broken the spell of my poetry."

The hum of voices began again, louder this time. No one said a word to hurt Mrs. McFee's feelings. And, of course, everyone made pretty speeches to Cousin Eva about her poems. The lady poet perked up and looked happy again.

Everyone raved about Mother's meringues and the flower mints from Atlanta. Everyone clapped loudly when Captain Jim gave Cousin Eva an ashtray of pure copper. "For the first lady brave enough to go underground in Isabella Mine," he said.

It had been a good party after all. The last guest left for home. Cousin Eva and Mother kicked off their slippers.

"Such happy memories of you and your mountains I will take home next week," Cousin Eva said.

"You're not going so soon!" Mother exclaimed.

"You've only been here a month," Daddy added. "No month is long enough to see all our mountain beauties."

"Why, William, it's November. You know as well as I do that I always make my Christmas fruitcakes in November. They must have time to mellow."

She would miss her poet cousin, Molly thought. Their spirits matched somehow, though there were years and years between them. Would Cousin Eva ever send them that promised poem about mountains? Perhaps not, for the flatlands are her country, Molly thought now. The mountains are mine.

8

CHRISTMAS TREE
HUNT

It had snowed in the night! When she looked out her window in the morning, Molly's heart skipped a beat. The snow wasn't deep. Only an inch or so of beautiful white coverlet lay on the ground. Today was Going-for-the-Tree Day. What if Daddy didn't dare drive the long five miles down Turtle Town Road? There, where forests covered Little Frog Mountain, every year they found the Christmas tree.

Daddy hadn't made up his mind. At breakfast, while eating pancakes with clover honey, he considered. While drinking a second cup of coffee, Daddy stared out the frosty window at the snow.

Molly and Ruth were mice holding their breath. They made gray, milky soup of their oatmeal, stirring and stirring. Penny, who had never been on the Christmas Tree Hunt, sang her favorite song:

Old Santa Claus is coming soon;
It's really Christmas-time.
I hear his sleighbells jingling far away.

Nobody reminded her that singing at the table isn't polite.

At last Molly burst out, "We can't have Christmas without a tree! Who's afraid of a little snow anyway?"

"Maybe it will melt by tomorrow," Mother said helpfully. Then she added, "Other people have sense enough to *buy* their trees."

This was true. Mountain people sold them on the street in Ducktown every year. These trees were often thin and scrawny. The Meade family liked to cut its own tree from forests that belonged to the Copper Company. Theirs was always the prettiest Christmas tree in Isabella Camp. Mother was as proud of it as anybody, but she was afraid of snow.

"Tomorrow is the Day Before Christmas." Daddy rolled his napkin into his ring and left the table. "I can't go for a tree then. We'll go today, just as we planned." Mother looked startled but said nothing.

Daddy's eyes were shining now. "Molly's right. Who's afraid of a little snow? My tires are good. If the road's slippery, I'll put on chains. Get your things on, girls." He had made up his mind.

So had Mother. And about some things Mother knew best.

"Penny is too little for a long walk through the woods, even without snow," she said now. "And Ruth certainly may *not* go on such a wild-goose chase. I heard her coughing in the night. You know as well as I do, William, that being exposed to snow is dangerous for children. It can even bring on pneumonia, my mother used to say." Then she saw Ruth's and Penny's disappointed faces.

"You'll be glad you stayed home," she comforted the little girls. "Vashti and I are going to make Christmas cookies. Ruth may make the pink and green frosting. Penny may trim the gingerbread men with currants and cinnamon drops."

Dressing for a trek through snow was an ordeal. It was almost (but not quite) enough to make Molly wish to stay home and make cookies, too. Her old plaid winter coat, already outgrown, was too tight with a sweater under it. Worse, this was a day when there was no getting out of wearing those horrible leggings.

Long ago, Molly had counted the rows of little black buttons up the sides. There were thirty-seven on each leg. For ten minutes no one could find the button hook.

(It was on the second shelf in the pantry, of all places!) Then Mother tied her own scratchy mohair scarf around Molly's neck. She insisted on two pairs of mittens. The old plaid tam must be pulled low over Molly's ears.

By now, it was almost impossible for Molly to move. So Daddy helped her squeeze into last winter's galoshes. Under them she wore two pairs of woolen socks. She felt like a stuffed doll with no joints.

Daddy sharpened his hatchet and put a saw and a tow sack into the car. Mother gave them a thermos bottle of hot soup.

"Promise me," she said to Daddy, "that you'll not go into the snowy woods. Just cut the first little evergreen you see growing beside the road. Then come right home."

Daddy was pulling on his own boots. Perhaps he hadn't heard Mother. Anyway, he didn't reply, Molly noticed. Then they were off, on the way to Turtle Town. It wasn't a town at all; just a turnoff, into the mountains where almost no one ever went. Two little faces watched forlornly through the kitchen window. Molly and Daddy waved.

The beautiful white world quite took Molly's breath away. Angellico Mountain was a sleeping giant under its snow blanket. Nearby hills were white sheep nestling close to each other to keep warm.

Daddy drove extra slowly. Molly was quiet. Driving on a snowy road was dangerous, she knew. They were alone in a white, silent world. All the way to Ducktown they passed only two creeping cars, then none.

"We're explorers in a strange land," Molly said at

last. "Maybe this is the way the North Pole looks."

Daddy grinned but didn't turn to look at her. His hands gripped the wheel, and his eyes never left the road. They skidded only once, just a little. At last they reached the Turtle Town turnoff. Here the snow was a little deeper. It was hard to see the edges of the road, and there were no tracks.

"We'll leave the car here," Daddy decided. "Walking is easier than driving today."

They piled out and began hiking. Not down the road, but into the forest where bare trees were like black lace against the snow. Daddy carried the saw and hatchet, Molly the tow sack.

They trudged through a fairyland that seemed hushed and frozen under some magic spell. Until now, no human foot had left its mark on the snow. Here and there, bird and rabbit tracks criss-crossed their path. These were like feather-stitching, Molly thought, on a pure white tablecloth. There was no sound, except the plop of stray chunks of snow falling from tree branches. Once a crow cawed loudly from the top of a sycamore tree. Perhaps he didn't like having two-legged creatures trespass on his forest kingdom.

I must write a poem about woods in snow, Molly thought. She had almost forgotten their errand, until Daddy spoke.

"I'm looking for a special tree marked in my mind's eye last summer," he said, "on the day we picked blue-berries near here."

"Everything looks different in winter when trees are bare," Molly said, "even when there's no snow. We'll never find one special tree."

She should have known Daddy better than that. His "mind's eye" was like a camera that took pictures to keep. They crossed a brook, sleeping under its thin mirror of ice. The ice shivered into tinkling splinters when Molly tested it.

"There's our tree!" Daddy shouted suddenly. Molly looked. Yes, it was a perfect little hemlock, meant to be a Christmas tree. Its dark green branches drooped under their weight of snow. Its tip would hold high a silver star.

"Oh, Daddy! It's beautiful!" Molly exclaimed. "Is it tall enough to touch the ceiling? Ruth and Penny will be disappointed if it doesn't."

"Well, I didn't happen to bring my tape measure," Daddy laughed. "But that tree looks just about right to my eye." Daddy's eye could be trusted in most matters.

So he took off his heavy jacket and set to work with hatchet and saw. He was like a woodman in a storybook, Molly thought. Most Isabella fathers couldn't find their way into and out of the forest, much less chop down a tree. Kate's father never hiked in the mountains. He wouldn't know a hemlock from an oak tree or a rabbit from a chipmunk, for that matter.

"Stay back, child!" Daddy commanded. "Let's not have an accident when it falls. I'd have a hard time deciding which to carry back to the car—you or the tree. I couldn't carry both; that's sure."

When it toppled, the tree was taller than Daddy. He tied a rope around its branches, then shouldered its trunk. The two explorers turned back toward the car. The tree's tip trailed in the snow behind them.

It would have been easy to follow their own footprints back to the road. But they didn't retrace their steps. Soon Molly saw the reason. It was another of Daddy's remembered landmarks. They came upon a holly bush, thick with bright red berries. When interrupted, a small flock of winter birds whirred away from their feast.

"Don't worry," Molly told them. "We won't take much of your berry dinner. Just a few branches." She and Daddy stuffed the tow sack with shining holly. They were glad of thick mittens to protect their hands from thorns.

Surely now it was time to find the car, Molly began to think. But no, Daddy was looking for mistletoe. Without it, no Christmas was complete. They stopped at last beneath a giant tulip tree. High in its bare branches perched clusters of green, like round bouquets. They were mistletoe.

"Oh, Daddy!" Molly cried. "You can't climb that high! It's dangerous! What would Mother say?"

Already Daddy had dropped the Christmas tree and was climbing from branch to branch, up and up. Below, Molly held her breath. "When I was a boy I could climb a greased pole," Daddy had often boasted. But now he and Molly were deep in the woods; who knew exactly where? What if he should fall? If he did, how on earth could she find help?

He didn't fall. Instead, Daddy cut and threw down bunch after bunch of mistletoe for Molly to catch.

"It's lovely!" she called up the tree. "It's a good berry year!" Last winter there had been no berries at all. This mistletoe was trimmed with tiny waxen pearls. It would hang, tied with red ribbon, in the front hall. A "kissing ball," some people called it. Stealing Kisses Under Mistletoe was a Christmas game everybody like to play.

"That's about it," Daddy said, when safely down. I guess it's time for home."

Though she didn't say so, Molly agreed. Suddenly the sun grew pale. Long blue shadows stretched beneath the trees. A chill wind shook sugar snow from the trees. In spite of all those heavy wraps, she was cold to the bone. Her fingers were numb. Were they frostbitten, she wondered? Worse than any of this, did Daddy know where they were? Molly shivered from cold, plus something she would not name, even to herself.

They trudged with heavy feet, Indian file. Carrying the sack of greens, Molly felt like a squaw following her brave.

"Do you know where we are?" she finally dared to ask.

"Why, of course I know!" Daddy sounded shocked. "Look ahead."

There was the faithful Studebaker, parked between two pines. She should have had more faith in Daddy's sense of direction, Molly thought. Sometimes other men got lost in the mountains when hunting or fishing. Daddy never did. They tied the Christmas tree to the top of the car and put the stuffed sack into the trunk.

"Let's try a sip of your mother's soup," Daddy remembered. "It ought to warm the cockles of our hearts." Which it did. Snuggled close to Daddy, lap robe tucked around her knees, Molly began to thaw. They started for home.

Through the frosty windshield, they watched the winter sun slide out of sight behind Big Frog Mountain.

Above it the western sky, Molly thought, was just the color of her turquoise ring. Big Frog itself matched Ruthie's amethyst. She felt snug and safe, for wasn't Daddy at the wheel? Even the wind, whistling through a crack in the car's snap-on curtains, could not make her shiver again.

No one saw them drive up to the back gate and untie the tree.

"Christmas is coming! The goose grows fat. Please put a penny in the old man's hat," Daddy sang loudly. He and Molly stamped snow from their boots and banged on the back door.

There was a flurry of welcoming kisses, with no need of mistletoe. There were hot baths and a hot supper of scalloped oysters and baked potatoes dripping with butter. There were the first samples of the holiday cookies. Molly ate a reindeer frosted with pink and a gingerbread man with currant buttons on his coat.

To everyone's delight, once set in its stand, their tree touched the ceiling. It smelled spicy, like the forest brought indoors for Christmas. Tree trimming began. There were:

> Fuzzy Santa dolls, with cotton fur
>   on their red flannel suits
> Spun glass balls, light as bubbles
> Velvet birds with silken tails
> Three empty cornucopias, to be filled
>   with candy by Old St. Nick
> China angels with gossamer wings
> A pleated fan
> A wooden rocking horse meant for an elf

> A little drummer boy
> Thick ropes of gold tinsel
> Silver icicles, too many to count.

On bottom branches, with a little help, Penny looped her own colored paper chains. Molly and Ruth hung popcorn strings. These looked like the real snow that had trimmed their tree when it lived outdoors, Molly thought.

Last, Daddy pinched a candle in its little holder on the end of every branch. High in the tree's tip he set the silver star that had been Mother's when she was a girl. Yes, theirs was the most beautiful Christmas tree ever.

"It's prettier than ours," Kate admitted next day when she saw it. "Our tree was the last one the peddler had to sell. It's a holly bush, not shaped like a tree at all. It hasn't a single berry either, and it hurts like anything to try to trim it around all those thorns. Your tree looks more like Christmas."

Molly looked at her in surprise. Why, Kate was jealous! She had never dreamed that Kate envied her anything. She thought of Vashti's words, "Jealous folks gets green eyes." Kate's eyes were as gray as ever, but it was nice for once to be a jump ahead of her enemy/best friend.

Then Molly remembered feeling sorry for Kate every year at Christmastime. The Tylers' tree was never beautiful. Kate's presents were never as wonderful as Molly's. Suddenly she felt a spark of the Spirit of Christmas.

"You may come look at our tree every single day, if you like," she said now. And Molly made up her mind

to give Kate the hand-painted desk set. To begin with, she had meant it to be Kate's Christmas present. But it was so pretty. Later she had been tempted to keep it for herself and give Kate a silly pin cushion.

After Kate left, the three sisters sat on the floor, admiring their tree.

"Which do you like best, the *Day Before* or *Christmas Day*?" Molly asked.

"I like them both best," Ruth said firmly.

"So do I," agreed Penny, who was a copycat.

So did Molly. On the *Day Before,* she liked:

>Sweet and spicy smells from the kitchen
>Trimming the mantel and doors with greens
>Singing carols around the piano
>Taking the box of toys and sweaters
>>to Mrs. Corn's grandchildren
>
>The Christmas Pageant at church
>>(This year she was going to be a Shepherd;
>>Kate a Wise Man)
>
>The suspense when stockings were hung
>>and it was time, for children everywhere,
>>to dream of Santa and sugar plums,
>>even though eleven-going-on-twelve years old.

Then there was *Christmas Day,* with its:

>Knobby stockings hanging by the fire and,
>>under the tree, too many presents to count
>
>Kisses and greetings and shouts of glee
>Neighbors in and out, come to share Christmas
>Candy and tangerines and almonds and stuffed,
>>sugary dates

Parents and sisters pleased with their presents,
   handmade in secret hours
Turkey oozing its stuffing and sweet potato pudding
   with marshmallows on top
Ambrosia for dessert and a slice
   of Cousin Eva's fruit cake
New games to try and puzzles enough
   to cover the floor
Seven new books (one of poems by John Keats)
And a new blue party dress with a swishy taffeta skirt.

No, she and Ruth and Penny could never decide which was the Best Day: the *Day Before* or *Christmas Day* itself.

One thing they did agree upon. The best part of Christmas was Lighting the Tree. This could happen only once each year, and at night. Even once was dangerous, Mother said. But she didn't say no, for she loved it, too.

A few Isabella people strung colored electric bulbs on their trees. These were something new, found only in Atlanta stores. Maybe they were safer, though not half so beautiful as real candlelight.

After a supper of cold turkey sandwiches and hot chocolate, the family gathered, not too near the tree. The three girls sat cross-legged on the rug. Mother was in her favorite chair, Vashti beside her. Daddy set up his stepladder, also two buckets—one of sand and one of water. He propped a broom nearby. They were for an emergency which surely wouldn't happen.

Then, with a long match, he lighted each candle. One by one the white tapers burst into living light.

Each, Molly thought, was a tiny star transplanted from the sky to their Christmas tree. It was a sight too beautiful for words. A picture in watercolor might be better than a poem. Still, how could any artist paint light from a hundred candles?

Was heaven half so lovely? she wondered. No one spoke. The Christmas tree seemed to breathe with shimmering light, soft and glowing. Shadows flickered on the wall. Molly was sure she would never, never forget this moment that came but once a year.

Too soon it was over.

"The candles are burning low, William," Mother warned. So Daddy climbed the ladder and snuffed them out, one by one. They sat in darkness for a long minute. Then someone snapped on a lamp. It looked harsh somehow, not soft like candlelight. But a lovely smell of melting wax filled the air.

"So goes another Christmas," Daddy said. He kissed Mother and picked up Penny. Wilted and droopy, she still clutched her new doll. Ruth, half-asleep, stumbled over the ruffle on her flannel nightgown.

Before Molly slipped into bed, she looked out her window. Above the rim of Angelico Mountain, a million stars shone like candles in a velvet sky. Which was the Christmas Star? she wondered. Next December she must study a map of the stars. Then she could pick it out. She must tie a string around her finger in the morning, so she wouldn't forget.

It didn't occur to Molly that the whole year until next Christmas was a long time to wear a string around her finger.

9

WILL YOU JOIN THE DANCE?

Molly watched a patch of sunlight dancing on the wall. It had stolen through a crack in the drawn window shade. Taking a nap in the afternoon made her feel like a baby. Even Penny didn't take naps anymore.

Of course, Penny didn't go to dances either; neither would Ruth for years and years yet. Mother had been firm. So had Kate's mother, which was a comfort. "No nap, no seeing the New Year in," they had decided.

This wasn't her and Kate's first dance. Isabella girls, after their tenth birthdays, went to the club dance every month. There was no dancing school in Isabella. So, unless their fathers taught them, how else would they learn the waltz and the fox trot? Someday, she and Kate would turn into young ladies. Who ever heard of a young lady who couldn't dance?

Until now, the two girls had been sent home to bed

at ten o'clock. But tonight was New Year's Eve. Tonight, for the first time, they were to be allowed to "dance the New Year in."

Her new blue taffeta dress hung waiting now on the closet door. Even in the dim room, the dress seemed to shimmer. "Seafoam blue," Mother called it. After a long look at herself in the mirror, Molly had decided that the color matched her eyes. The skirt swished when she moved. Like a real young lady's dancing dress, it dipped fashionably in the back. It was a lovely dress.

There was too much to think about for Molly to sleep. Instead, she shut her eyes and tried to imagine what it would be like when 1930 turned into 1931.

After supper it took Mother forever to dress.

"Who wants to arrive early at a dance?" she asked.

I do, Molly thought. She tried her best to sit still in Mother's little rocker and not wrinkle her taffeta skirt. She watched Mother twist her long dark hair into a knot and put rouge on her cheeks. Daddy paced the floor and twirled his watch chain.

When they arrived at the club, music was pouring from the Victrola. It was the lovely record of "Louise." Lights blazed. Several couples were already dancing. The club looked beautiful in its holiday trimmings. Streamers of red and green paper hung over the dancers' heads, Christmas bells over doors and windows. The Tylers were there first, which Molly had been sure would happen.

Kate was wearing her new Christmas dress, too. It was really new, not a leftover from her big sister. And it was green. Kate almost always wore green.

"It goes so well with the child's auburn hair," Mrs.

Tyler often remarked. The dress was too long, Molly thought now. It hung way below Kate's knees all around and made her look like a little old lady.

Mrs. Tyler liked for Kate's skirts to be "long enough to grow to." Molly was glad Mother added ruffles to her outgrown skirts, so they were never too long and never too short. Still, Kate's dress *was* pretty, and it did go well with her red hair.

The two girls hugged each other and whispered, "I like your Christmas dress." They said it at exactly the same time. So they locked little fingers, closed their eyes, and made wishes.

I wish *St. Nicholas* magazine would print my "Fire on the Mountain" poem, Molly thought. Wishes, of course, could never be spoken aloud—certainly not to Kate, who laughed at poems.

It was time to dance with fathers. Mrs. Tyler and Mother settled themselves in chairs against the wall. Isabella mothers seemed to enjoy watching their daughters learn how to dance.

The music was a waltz. Molly counted, "One-two-three, one-two-three," to herself. She tried to remember to slide gracefully on "three."

"Don't be so stiff," Daddy said under his breath in her ear. He and Molly waltzed around the dance floor. "Relax. I'll guide you."

Molly tried her best to relax. She tried not to think of her feet. This was hard, for Daddy sometimes stepped on them. Worse than that, he bounced when he danced. When Mother gently complained about this, he always said, "Bouncing is the difference between walking and dancing." Molly had noticed that Mother leaned heavily on his shoulder to hold Daddy down, when they danced together.

Bouncing was better than walking, which was Mr. Tyler's idea of how to dance. When it was their turn on the floor, Kate's father pushed Molly into a stiff one-two-three walk. It wasn't dancing at all.

Someone changed the record to "Valencia." This music was a swinging fox trot. A few dancers tried to tango. She and Mr. Tyler would have to *run* to keep up. Just then Mr. McFee touched Molly's hand and asked politely, "May I have this dance?"

Mr. McFee was always nice to Kate and her. He never once said, "What pretty little girls we have here!" or "How grown-up you look tonight!" Instead, he made them feel like real young ladies. Besides, he was the best dancer in Isabella. And tonight he had chosen Molly ahead of Kate!

He swept her into his arms and onto the dance floor. With Mr. McFee, Molly could forget about counting. Her nose rubbed against the buttons on his vest. But he lifted Molly so that her feet seemed to dance by themselves. They dipped and swooped, like swallows in the evening air. It was like playing a gavotte on the piano, Molly thought. Except that feet were dancing, instead of fingers.

The music stopped much too soon. Next, someone chose a record of Dixieland jazz. Mr. Tooker twirled pretty Miss Hall onto the floor. Everyone stopped to watch, for not many people could dance the new Charleston. Heels and toes flew. The fringe on Miss Hall's red skirt shimmered and shook. It quite took Molly's breath away.

I'll never learn to dance the Charleston, she thought in despair. Not in a million years.

Then it was over. The next record was "Oh, Them Golden Slippers." This was everybody's favorite, for it made feet dance all by themselves.

"Time for a Paul Jones!" Mr. McFee said loudly. "Ladies to the right. Gentlemen to the left. Now choose your partners!"

This sometimes meant a quick turn with a handsome young man—one who didn't usually look at girls who were eleven-going-on-twelve.

"Back to back!" Mr. McFee called.

That was fun and often caused mix-ups.

"Do-si-do, and sashay down the middle!" Then, "Now let's have the ladies throw their right shoes into the center!"

This was something new. It took only a minute to unstrap a Mary Jane shoe.

"Now, gentlemen, find your lady's slipper. Cinderellas all!"

What a scramble! This time it was Kate who drew a prize partner. The young man had curly hair and a teasing smile. Molly found herself walking to music again with Mr. Tyler.

Then she had a turn with Mr. Bradford, who held her too tightly against his big stomach. Molly could feel her dress hike up high in the back. Maybe her skirt should have had one more ruffle, or been long like Kate's. She could feel her knee socks slipping into baggy wrinkles. Why were her garters always weak?

After the Paul Jones, someone put on a quiet record. Molly was out of breath and hot. She and Kate sat in "wallflower chairs" to rest.

"I'm going for a drink of water," Molly decided. She opened the swinging door and stepped into the club kitchen. There she forgot the water. For, sitting on the kitchen table, were Miss Hall and her dancing partner. They were kissing each other! Molly felt herself blush all over. The lovers sprang apart.

"Don't go!" Miss Hall said. She looked as calm as a cucumber. She waved the cigarette in her right hand. "We won't bite. Surely you've seen people kiss before. If you haven't, it's high time you did!"

Without even an "excuse me, please," Molly backed out fast. She went to the powder room, which was empty. There she washed her face in cold water. In a minute Kate found her.

"What on earth's the matter?" she asked. "Do you have rouge on your cheeks? They're awfully red."

So Molly told her, after making Kate swear on a stack of Bibles never to tell about the kiss in the kitchen.

"What's wrong with a kiss between lovers?" Kate asked.

"Why, Mr. Tooker has just been working two weeks for the Copper Company!" Molly was shocked. "They're not even engaged. You don't kiss somebody until you're going to be married to him. I'm sure my mother never did, and I won't either!"

Kate put on her wise look.

"What a baby you are!" she said scornfully. "I asked my mother once. She said she kissed three other men before she even met my father. I bet your mother did, too."

Molly said nothing. A club dance wasn't the place for a quarrel. Besides, she had to think about lovers and kisses for a while. Was she really, as Kate was forever saying, a silly and a baby?

It was ten o'clock. Time for parents to dance together. Molly and Kate had to dance with each other if they were to dance at all. They took turns leading. Molly had to admit that Kate was good at this. Though girls weren't supposed to lead, she was easy to follow.

Every few minutes the girls stopped at the refreshment table for a cup of punch. In it they tasted pineapple juice and ginger ale. Cranberry juice made it red. There were also cookies of all kinds: meringue kisses, chocolate drops, coconut squares, and pecan tassies.

"Don't be greedy with the cookies," their mothers had warned. As if they didn't know party manners. So Molly and Kate kept count. They ate only six cookies each. That didn't seem too many for a whole evening of dancing.

Before they knew it was so late, someone shouted, "Five minutes to twelve!" Someone else stopped the music. Dancers froze. Everyone watched the hands of the clock on the wall. Was it always this quiet just before the Old Year died? Then the clock began to strike —nine, ten, eleven, TWELVE!

"Happy New Year!" everybody shouted. Horns appeared from pockets. Someone blew a shrill whistle. What a din! Mr. McFee began singing "Auld Lang Syne." Everyone chimed in, even people who couldn't sing in tune.

She had been wrong about kissing, Molly decided. For all sorts of grown-ups began kissing each other. It was just as if kissing between friends were an everyday matter. Parents, too, of course. She expected that. But a few men were kissing ladies who were *not* their wives. And two young ladies were locked in their partners' arms, too tightly for any proper dance.

It was "Oh, Them Golden Slippers" again. From somewhere, balloons and paper hats appeared, as if by magic. Kate's was an owl's face; hers an Uncle Sam hat, with stripes and stars. The dance floor was crowded with merry, noisy people behaving like children.

It would be nice to be taller, Molly decided. She and Kate couldn't half see where they were going. She could hardly recognize the other dancers anyway. This was partly because of the silly hats and masks. There were grinning clowns, queens with gilt tiaras, soldiers. An evil-looking wolf was dancing with Red Riding Hood. The Seven Dwarfs held hands and danced in a ring. Daddy was Old St. Nick, with a cherry for a nose and a long white beard. He was bouncing happily with Mother, who wore a domino mask.

Everyone acted strangely, as if they had forgotten who they were. Would they remember their real selves tomorrow? Miss Hall was dancing in her stocking feet. Mrs. Tyler stepped on the hem of her dress and ripped it. As if it didn't matter, she pinned it up with a hairpin and kept dancing. Mr. Miller swayed and lurched in the strangest way.

"He probably spiked his punch in the kitchen," Kate said in Molly's ear. Spiked punch at a Copper Company dance was against the rules. Everybody knew that. Yet tonight no one seemed to mind. How could something be wrong at other times but at a New Year's Dance be smiled about?

So this was what "dancing in the New Year" meant. Grown-ups could behave like naughty children. Old rules and manners died with the Old Year. Tomorrow Molly would have to do some thinking. Who could think in the middle of a carnival?

At half-past twelve someone forgot to wind the Victrola. The music whined to a stop. Dancing stopped, too, for suddenly everyone seemed to wilt. Miss Hall looked, Molly thought, like a doll that had lost its stuffing. The party was over. Mother and Daddy and Molly drove quietly home in the cold winter dark.

"Well," Daddy said, "everybody had a rousing good time. I'm sure I did."

"A few had too good a time," Mother remarked. "There may be some aching heads in the morning, and a few regrets. Did Molly enjoy seeing her first New Year in, I wonder?" Then, for Molly didn't answer, "Why, the dear child is asleep."

Molly wasn't really asleep. Through half-closed eyes she was staring out the car window. Moon and sky and stars looked the same as ever. She was a little disappointed. The first night of a New Year ought to look a little different. Would the rest of 1931 be just like old 1930, she wondered? Yes, she had some thinking to do. Thoughts that she didn't mean to share with Kate, or anybody else, for that matter. Unless she put them in a poem someday.

10

LITTLE POTATO CREEK

At eleven o'clock in the morning, Miss Alice turned on the schoolroom lights. A storm was brewing in the mountains. Through the east windows Molly could see dark clouds piling up over Angelico Mountain. Now and then lightning flashed in the distance. Thunder rumbled far away.

Molly and Kate sat in the back corner of the schoolroom, behind the littlest children's sand table. In whispers to each other, they were reciting the Preamble to the Constitution of the United States. After lunch they were to say it to Miss Alice.

Today Molly found it hard to keep her mind on a dull civics lesson. Four third-grade children were saying the seven times table out loud. They almost made a song of "Six times seven is forty-two. Seven times seven is forty-nine." While they recited, Miss Alice kept one eye on Tommy and Susan, the first-grade twins, and Della Frye. They were writing rows of capital *B*'s on the blackboard in yellow chalk. Other children were reading quietly at their desks. All except Ruthie. Molly noticed that her sister was staring at the brown and white picture of the Pilgrim Fathers that hung over Miss Alice's desk. What was Ruth dreaming about? she wondered.

"When in the Course of human events, it becomes necessary for one people to dissolve. . . ." Molly stumbled and forgot what came next.

". . . it becomes necessary for one people to dissolve *the political bands* . . ." Kate prompted her. "Now let me try it. I said the whole Preamble to my father last night without a single mistake."

She said it again now, flipping her hair out of her eyes and smiling smugly.

Kate's hair is *red*, not auburn, Molly thought for the hundredth time. And her face has a thousand freckles. Someday, when I'm mad enough, I'm going to tell her so.

Aloud she said crossly, "I hate civics. Who wants to know the Preamble of the Constitution by heart? I'd rather memorize a poem any day. Part of 'The Lady of Shalott'—that part about:

> And sometimes through the mirror blue
> The knights come riding two and two.

Or some of Cousin Eva's poetry." Best of all, she thought but didn't say it out loud, was writing poems of her own.

Kate was feeling snippy, almost rude this morning. Maybe the coming storm was upsetting her.

"Your cousin doesn't write real poetry at all," she whispered now. "Whoever heard of poems that don't rhyme?"

"My cousin writes *free verse*," Molly replied stiffly. "Free verse doesn't have to rhyme, but it sounds like poetry when you read it out loud." Then she said airily, "Sometime I *may* let you see her book. It's called *River Acres*. The poems are all about flat country, where nobody ever saw a mountain. Cousin Eva gave me my very own copy."

"I don't give a fig for poetry that doesn't rhyme," Kate whispered back. She didn't like any kind of poetry, Molly knew. Kate preferred reading books with lots of action—stories about explorers and pirates mostly, and Sherlock Holmes mysteries.

"Are you two girls really studying together?" Miss Alice asked sharply. "If not, please return to your desks."

Miss Alice's voice was almost never sharp.

"She has more patience than anyone I've ever known," Molly's mother often said. "Imagine being shut up in that school every day with fifteen children of such different ages. Why, this year there are six grades to teach, in one room."

"It must be like juggling oranges to keep them all busy and quiet and learning. She's really a marvel," other parents agreed.

But today Miss Alice wasn't her usual patient self. Something was upsetting her. She kept gazing out the window toward Angelico Mountain. Not that a storm in

early spring was anything unusual. Still, the sky was awfully black. Thunder rumbled louder and louder. Flashes of lightning crackled sharply. The littlest children hid their faces on their desk tops.

Molly looked up from her geography book, then poked Kate to look, too. Angelico Mountain had disappeared in a curtain of dark clouds. Gusts of wind rattled the schoolroom windows. A moving wall of rain was coming closer and closer to Isabella Camp. It happened so fast. Suddenly the rain was like a herd of horses galloping toward them. Miss Alice stopped the lessons.

"Though it's not Friday, we'll have our singing time now," she said. The children gathered around the piano. Miss Alice played *fortissimo*, and everyone sang loudly to match. They sang "She'll Be Coming Round the Mountain When She Comes" and "Skip to My Lou, My Darling."

"Let's sing 'It Ain't Gonna Rain No Mo',' " Jack McFee suggested. Everyone laughed. What a good idea!

> It ain't gonna rain, it ain't gonna snow,
> It ain't gonna rain no mo',
> Come on ev'rybody now,
> It ain't gonna rain no mo'.

They sang as loudly as they could. Still, they sounded drowned and thin, Molly thought, like forlorn, lost children. For all the while, the storm was roaring just outside like a freight train.

Lights flickered, then went out, leaving the schoolroom in a dim half light. The little children began to sob. Molly and Kate, being the eldest, tried to help Miss Alice soothe them.

Then, gradually, the storm, like most quick mountain storms, roared away among the hills into the distance. It was like the game of ninepins in the Rip Van Winkle story, Molly thought. The noise rolled farther and farther away. At last, it was only an echo.

"Well!" Miss Alice said brightly. She settled a stray hairpin and straightened her crocheted collar. "Thank goodness that's over." Then she looked outside and grew paler than before. "Children!" she commanded. "Come look at Little Potato Creek."

They crowded at the windows. Their usually gentle, shallow stream was a raging torrent of red-mud-colored water. It filled the wide valley between the schoolhouse and the other half of Isabella Camp on the opposite hill. Every gully was pouring its own small river into Little Potato Creek, which was no longer little.

The Miller home sat on the opposite hilltop. Suddenly Robbie Miller yelled, "Look! That's my Snooker's house!" As the children watched, almost afraid to breathe, Snooker's small red doghouse tipped over in a gust of wind. Slowly at first, then faster and faster, it toppled down the hill. It was like a child's block that has been pushed.

"What if my dog's inside?" Robbie wailed.

"Now, Robbie," Miss Alice tried to soothe him. "Haven't you told us lots of times that Snooker is afraid of thunder? I'm sure your mother let him in your own house long ago."

Robbie stopped crying. He and the others watched as Snooker's house settled on one corner at the foot of the hill. There it rested, gingerly propped against a large rock.

There was more excitement. The rain stopped, but the creek was still angry. As they watched, horrified, their little footbridge keeled over on its side. Its posts had been washed away. Wild currents of water picked it up and rolled the bridge end over end. The children's own sturdy little bridge looked like a toothpick in the wild water.

"What will we do?" Ruthie cried. "How will we ever get home with no bridge? We can't wade through all that muddy water."

"We'll have to wait for the creek to go down," Miss Alice said cheerfully. Molly wondered if she really felt cheerful inside. Suppose it were tomorrow before the creek went down?

"We won't be going home for lunch today," their teacher told the children. "We'll have an indoor picnic instead. I've kept a little food stored away, in case this very thing should happen."

Miss Alice unlocked her supply closet. From its top shelf she took four cans of tomato soup, a saucepan, and a can opener. The children watched as she lit a spirit lamp and set the soup over its flame. Imagine it. Miss Alice could cook without a kitchen when she had to. Then she opened a box of crackers and a jar of peanut butter.

Four children had brought apples for the teacher that morning.

"Into how many pieces must I cut each apple?" Miss Alice asked. "There are sixteen of us, counting me."

Ruthie waved her hand. She had just been learning division in arithmetic.

"Into four pieces each," she said. Molly was proud of her for doing the problem in her head.

Then Robbie surprised everyone.

"I brought a bag of chocolate kisses today, for recess." He pulled them from his knickers pocket. Inside their silver foil, the candy was only a little melted. Robbie counted the kisses carefully into each child's hand. There were three for each and two for Miss Alice. It was a good picnic.

By now the sun had come out. Over Big Frog Mountain in the west, there hung a full rainbow. It was a perfect arc, with a fainter double. So they had an art lesson in painting rainbows. Some used crayons; some watercolors. The little children finger-painted their pictures. Miss Alice strung the fifteen rainbows across the top of the blackboard, where they looked beautiful.

Though the storm was over, no one felt like having ordinary lessons. This was no ordinary day. All were listening to the roar of Little Potato Creek, which was still a raging river. How would they get home, those who lived on the other side of Little Potato Creek? What would they eat for supper if they had to stay here? More of Miss Alice's emergency soup? Would they have to spend the night at school, without beds or blankets? And how could they let their mothers know they were safe? Mothers had such a habit of worrying.

So they had an Indoor Field Day. They played Simon Says and Drop the Handkerchief. Molly and Kate, being tallest, held hands to make a London Bridge to catch the little ones.

They went out on the porch for recess. Water still dripped from the schoolhouse roof, but Little Potato Creek looked less angry now. It had begun to shrink.

"Why can't we go home now?" Janey Harris asked. "Six of us live on this side of the creek, so we don't have to cross it."

"Let's wait and see," Miss Alice said. "There may be a washout or two on your path home. After a storm like this one, there's no telling how the gullies may have changed their courses. You wouldn't like slipping into one or finding it too wide to cross." So they played Corner Tag for a while, with porch posts for Home Free bases.

At half-past four by the school clock, the children were tired of games. Robbie had begun to tease the little girls. Peter Collins began to blow his bird whistle, which was against the rules. Miss Alice's hair was losing its pins, and her collar was decidedly crooked.

Little Della, who after all was only six, hid her face in Miss Alice's skirt and began to sob, "I want to go home! I want my mama!"

Just then there was a knock on the schoolroom door. It was Della's father.

"To the rescue!" Mr. Frye said, smiling. In his arms he carried a laundry bag stuffed with rubbers.

"I went to every house on this side of the creek, collecting these," he told them. "The path is slippery but safe enough for you children to walk home with me. There's only one washout. Those of you with long legs can jump it. I'll carry the little ones across."

"How about us? We live on the other side of Little Potato Creek. What shall we do?" Robbie asked. His chin, Molly noticed, was trembling.

"Stay right where you are and be patient," Mr. Frye told them firmly. "The creek will be back to normal soon. Have you looked at it lately? Your fathers are testing the car bridge now, to see if it will carry the weight of a car."

So Mr. Frye and six of the children left for the walk to their homes. The rest felt a little forlorn, but not for long. At five o'clock two cars crept slowly along the cinder road toward the school. Both stopped at the play yard gate.

"It's our daddies!" Molly shouted. She and Ruthie

and Kate hugged each other and danced up and down. There were the dear old Studebaker and the Tyler family's roadster.

"Here we are at last!" Mr. Tyler said. Both fathers were grinning like Cheshire cats. They kissed their own three daughters and the other girls besides. They shook hands warmly with Miss Alice. She looked, Molly thought, as happy as if the two men were *her* fathers.

Half the children, and their teacher, too, piled into the roadster, the rest into the Studebaker. The cars turned carefully around, then drove slowly around the curve of the nearest hill. Cinders had been washed away from most of the road, leaving it muddy and slippery.

It was half a mile to the car bridge across Little Potato Creek. The water had gone down amazingly. It was still the color of thick red mud, but the creek no longer roared. Once at the car bridge, both fathers stopped their automobiles.

"Everybody out!" Molly's father commanded. "We've tested the bridge and think it will take the weight of a car. But we'll take no chances. You children must walk across. We'll drive the cars over later."

So, holding hands (and breath), they walked single file across the plank bridge. The fathers carried the littlest children, one by one. Miss Alice held the railing and stepped lightly on tiptoe. Did she think her weight would break the bridge? Molly wondered. Tiny Miss Alice!

At last they were all safely across. Then Mr. Meade and Mr. Tyler returned to their cars and drove them slowly, slowly over the bridge. It was like the Billy Goats Gruff. Little Potato Creek, the wicked gnome, was waiting to gobble them up if they fell in.

"Our daddies are heroes," Molly said to Kate, just before stepping into the Studebaker to go home.

"Mine was more of a hero than yours," Kate replied with a quick toss of her head. "He drove our car over the bridge first. It might have broken, you know."

For once Molly said nothing at all. The adventure was over. How long would it be, she wondered, before there was a new footbridge across Little Potato Creek? Maybe there wouldn't be any school tomorrow. But already the creek was almost its innocent self again, almost shallow enough to wade.

MOUNTAIN FUNERAL

Ruth and Penny were playing with the rabbits in the backyard. They were not to let Foxy and Snowball nibble Daddy's parsley, nor taste a single bud from his sweet-smelling wallflowers.

Molly was curled on the window seat of the playroom, reading. This was her favorite nook in all the house. Its sunny windows looked out at Daddy's pansies. On this early spring day, these were in bright bloom. The purple, blue, and yellow of their flower faces were like a velvet robe spread over the garden bed.

Molly wasn't thinking of pansies just now. She was lost in her book. It was Volume IX of the *Junior Classics*, called *Myths and Legends*. The story was about a boy of ancient Greece, named Icarus. More than anything, he longed to fly like a bird. How wonderful it would be, he thought, to dip and swoop, to sail and soar on the wind. This was something no man or boy in all the world had ever done.

To please his son, Icarus' father made him a pair of wax wings. Wearing them, Icarus found to his joy that he could fly like an eagle—high in the heavens, close to the sun.

Why, it was the same sun that my giant still tosses over Angelico Mountain every morning, Molly marveled. The very same sun-ball for all those trillion years since Icarus lived in Greece!

It was not a happy myth. Alas, poor Icarus flew too near the sun. It melted his wax wings. The poor boy fell into the sea and was drowned. It was only a myth, a kind of fairy tale. But Molly's heart ached to think of the beautiful Greek lad dead. He had dared so much, then lost all.

To cheer herself up, Molly looked out the window at the pansies. Just then Vashti burst into the playroom. She was all a-fluster.

"Miss Molly!" she said. "You've just got to come quick. They's some man at the back door wants to see you."

"Who is it?" Molly asked.

"He says he's Sol, one of old Miz Corn's grandsons. I didn't let him in my kitchen, not with his muddy feet and dirty overhalls. But you'd better come see what he wants. I done hooked the screen door, so you'll be safe. Your ma's at a party at Miz Cutler's house. She wouldn't want you talkin' to the likes of this here hillbilly. But I'll stay close by to watch out for you."

Molly was curious. She uncurled her legs, which

were stiff from being sat on. She pulled up her knee socks and followed Vashti to the kitchen. Yes, it was one of the mountain men. He was twisting his limp hat in grimy hands. His hair hung over his eyes like a curtain. He looked at his shoes, not at Molly.

"I reckon as how you wouldn't know me," he said awkwardly. "I'm one of Maggie Corn's grandboys, name o' Sol. My grandmaw, she up and died last night."

Molly gasped. Mrs. Corn dead? It didn't seem possible. Why, just yesterday the woman had rattled by the back gate in her husband's wagon. Molly had seen her, huddled on a pile of rags, while old Mr. Corn yelled at the slow oxen.

"I'm so sorry," Maggie managed to stammer. Her thoughts whirled like a cloud of gnats. What would Mother say or do, if she were here? Why had Maggie Corn's grandson asked to tell his news to an eleven-year-old girl who wasn't even twelve yet?

Sol Corn cleared his throat and spoke again.

"My grandmaw, she allus said as how you could play the pianer right purty. We was wonderin' if'n you could play the organ at her funeral. It's gonna be at the Hopewell Gospel Church Sattidy, at noontime. Me and the fambly, we'd be right obleeged if'n you could do it."

Molly felt her eyes grow wide, then misty. She had been right. Old Mrs. Corn had loved beautiful things, though she never owned a string of beads or a pretty dress in all her life. Or lived in anything but a tumble-down cabin, a whoop and a holler from a neighbor. Still, Molly remembered now, there had been red geraniums and pink balsam blooming in lard cans on her rickety porch railing. And Maggie Corn had cocked an ear to Molly's piano practise while scrubbing floors on her hands and knees.

"I'll be glad to play the organ at her funeral," she told the limp and ragged man. He had not once looked into her eyes. Mrs. Corn would have called him "floopy," as she did wilted lettuce. "That is, if my parents say it's all right."

Sol Corn slid down the back steps without another word.

"Well!" Vashti came to the door, her hands white with flour. "What will yer ma and pa say to that, I wonder? They ain't likely to want you goin' to a fun'ral. Them mountain folks is rough and wildlike. You couldn't pay me to go. They wouldn't want me nohow, 'cause I'm black."

So there was a family conference at the supper table. Mother had doubts about the whole idea. So did Molly, though she didn't say so. What would it be like to see someone dead? Still, not every girl was asked to play the organ at a funeral. Kate would be astonished when she heard.

"The child has never been exposed to death," Mother said. "A mountain funeral will shock her. Hill people can be wild in their grief."

"Mrs. Corn was fond of Molly," Daddy said thoughtfully. "Poor soul. She had little enough pleasure in her hard life. The least we can do is let Molly play the organ at her funeral. We won't be doing it for that good-for-nothing husband of hers. Or for those ungrateful children. They all let her work her fingers to the bone for them."

"May I go, too?" Ruth asked, though not as if she really meant it.

"Certainly not!" Mother replied firmly. "Maybe Vashti will let you and Penny have cambric tea and cookies with your dolls while we're gone."

So it was decided. Daddy and Mother would drive Molly to the church. With them there, she would feel braver. No one thought to ask if she could make music come from the organ. She didn't intend to tell anybody she had already played it once.

What to play was a problem. It should be something solemn and slow. Then Molly remembered learning Chopin's "Funeral March" last summer. The very thing! It was sad and beautiful music. She would also sight-read hymns from the faded book on the organ's music rack. Probably no one had touched it since she and Kate had climbed into the church.

What did one wear to a funeral? Mother decided for her.

"You must wear your navy-blue sailor dress," she said. Molly hated that dress. It was wool and it scratched. "With a white tie, not the red one." As for herself, Mother took the sparkly beads off her own black poplin dress. She also ripped the red bird's wing from the brim of her black hat.

Kate was speechless at the news. Then she swallowed her envy and, as usual, had a good idea.

"Let's make a wreath of your father's pansies for the funeral. Mrs. Corn liked flowers. I know how to make a wreath with a coat hanger and some wire."

So, after school on Friday, the two girls worked on

the wreath. They twisted the hanger into a circle, then tied green periwinkle vines thickly around it. It was like making a holly wreath, except easier, for periwinkle had no thorns. At the last minute, so the blossoms wouldn't wither, they would stick bright pansies among the waxy leaves.

Mother found a purple ribbon from a candy box to tie on the finished wreath. It was beautiful. If she could look down from heaven, Mrs. Corn would be pleased. That night Molly dreamed of the old woman's wrinkled face. Though it still looked like a withered apple, in the dream her faded blue eyes were crinkled in a smile.

But next morning something made Molly slower than usual. It took forever to eat her bowl of oatmeal, even with brown sugar sprinkled on it. She put on her petticoat backward and, to save her life, couldn't make a proper sailor's knot in the white silk tie. Ruth finally came to her rescue.

Molly knew what was wrong. She wasn't a whit worried about playing the organ. That would be easy. But what would it be like to see Mrs. Corn dead? Though the sun was shining brightly, today the world seemed shadowy. Daddy had to honk twice before Molly was ready to hop into the car.

It hadn't rained in days, so Potato Creek was shallow enough to ford without getting stuck in mud.

It isn't far to the church, Molly thought. We might have walked. Then she giggled to herself, remembering the secret hike with Kate. Imagine Mother stepping from stone to stone across Potato Creek in high-heeled pumps! Mother wouldn't be caught dead crossing a stream on foot.

Today the rough hillside around Hopewell Gospel Church looked different. Scattered among patches of broomsedge were a few rusty flivvers, a buggy with a drooping horse, and two ox wagons. A sway-backed mule was tied to a hitching post. The Studebaker looked lonely, like a slick new bird in a flock of scraggly crows.

Not for long. Around the bend of the road, here came Kate and her father in their new roadster with the top down. So now there were two shiny cars parked side by side.

What had made Kate come? Was it curiosity or a kind of sadness for old Mrs. Corn? Whatever had brought her, Molly was glad. Seeing Kate was like slipping into comfortable shoes after trying to walk in new ones that hurt a little.

"I can't sit with you," Molly whispered as the girls went up the sagging church steps. "I have to sit on the organ bench the whole time. You can hold our pansy wreath."

"I know," Kate replied. She squeezed Molly's hand. Today her eyes were not at all green. Maybe playing for a funeral was something Kate didn't envy her. Molly's knees suddenly felt weak, as if she had been running for miles. She slipped her hand into Daddy's. Mother looked at her anxiously.

"Are you sure you want to do this?" she asked. "You look a little pale, dear."

"Of course I do," Molly said firmly. She lifted her chin and walked through the church door.

Hopewell Gospel Church was half filled with mountain folk. Their heads turned to stare at the Isabella

Camp people. No one nodded a greeting. No one spoke. Daddy, still holding Molly's hand, led her to the front of the church.

There the organ sat on a low platform near the pulpit. Molly slid onto the organ bench. It faced the people. She fumbled with her music and opened the faded hymnbook.

"Can you really play this thing?" Daddy asked. He looked at the organ as if it were some strange animal that might bite.

"Of course I can," Molly said airily.

Daddy patted her on the shoulder. Then he returned to the back pew to sit with Mother, Mr. Tyler, and Kate. Their clothes, though properly dark for a funeral, looked out of place. They were like the shiny cars outside. For the hill people, even in their Sunday best, were patched and poor.

The Corn family sat on the mourners' bench up front. The oldest daughter, Nance, was there, in a droopy calico dress that had once been pink. Molly knew Nance. She had often knocked at the back door and begged money for a bag of Little Mule snuff. Of course Mother never gave it to her. Instead, she often gave the woman a sack of sugar and a piece of fatback to boil with turnip greens. Last week she had given her an old sweater, a ham hock, and some laundry soap. Every Christmas, Molly and her sisters took a basket of good things—cookies, warm clothes, and outgrown toys —to Nance's children. There was a new baby every year.

Today Nance was holding the newest baby in her arms. Mrs. Corn would have said it looked "porely."

The older children sat staring straight ahead. One had his thumb in his mouth and was drooling. Maybe they are frightened, too, Molly thought. They are also sad that their grandmother is dead—if they know what "dead" means.

Old Mr. Corn sat quietly between two of his seven sons. His long arms dangled between his knees. He looked bewildered, as if his thoughts were fuzzy. Molly hoped he hadn't taken a swig of moonshine whiskey before coming to his wife's funeral. Sol, sitting behind his grandfather, was wearing a stiff new pair of overalls. He caught Molly's eye, and one corner of his mouth twitched.

A long pine box stood on saw horses just below the pulpit. Seeing it, Molly grew cold all over. Like a thunderclap, it dawned on her that Old Mrs. Corn was in that box! It held her dead body!

At that instant, a strange man burst like a cyclone through the church door. He was tall and thin—a pale scarecrow, Molly thought. He wore a rusty frock coat and a flowing tie. He went straight to the pulpit, set down an enormous Bible, then leaned over Molly.

"I'm Preacher Org Boggs," he said. "I take it you're the little lady who's going to help us praise the good Lord with song."

Molly nodded dumbly. She hadn't tried the organ yet, to see if it would make any sound at all today.

Preacher Boggs spoke loudly into Molly's ear. "Let's begin with that good old hymn, 'When the Roll Is Called Up Yonder, I'll Be There.' That ought to pump a little spirit into the mourners. It's number fifty-six."

Molly found the music. She began pushing the organ's pedals to force air into its pipes. She held her breath.

Keep pumping, she told herself. Remember, it's just like swimming. Feet and hands move together in rhythm. If I forget either one, the music will drown.

She tried the first notes of the hymn. A wheezy sound came out, more like a squeaky gate than music. There was a rattle in the pedals. Just like last summer, the F-sharp didn't sound at all. Molly played the whole first verse. Yes, she could do it, even without the F-sharp, as long as she didn't stop pumping.

Preacher Boggs began to sing, his voice like a hoarse frog's. A few other voices joined him timidly. By the fourth verse, the whole congregation was singing—some in tune, some not. Nobody kept up with the organ. Instead, Molly had to keep up with them. A few people waved their arms and began to moan. Some rocked and swayed, as if in a trance. Somebody shouted, "Hallelujah!" Someone answered, "Amen!"

Was this the way to act at a funeral? There wasn't time to think about it now. When Molly stopped pumping the pedals, the music died with a last wheeze. Preacher Boggs began to preach.

"Brethren and Sistern!" he shouted. His voice was like a trumpet. "We have done come together to say good-bye to Maggie Corn. She were a good wife, a loving mother, a kind granny, and a friend to you and I. This woman lived and dwelt among us for upwards of four score years. That's a mighty long time to live and dwell upon this old earth. (Some would call it this Vale of Tears.)

"But rest you assured, when the roll is called up yonder, Sister Corn will be there, among the saints. (I pause to ask you—when *you* knock on those Pearly Gates, will good St. Peter open them for *you*? Are you washed in the blood of the Lamb?)"

Someone on the mourners' bench began to sob quietly. Molly tried not to look, but she couldn't help it. One of the seven Corn sons was wiping his eyes with a dirty rag. Nance's baby had begun to wail. An older child sat on the floor, tearing pages from a hymnbook. No one noticed him. Old Mr. Corn's head was nodding. Molly was horrified. Somebody ought to shake the man. How could he doze at his own wife's funeral?

The sermon went on forever. Preacher Boggs was wound up like a jumping jack. His arms waved and his legs jerked. Molly stopped listening to his words. Her head buzzed like a wasps' nest.

Later she would remember hearing bits like "that old man Devil," "Repent, my children, before it's too late!" and "the fires of Hell!" Preacher Boggs's face flamed. Perspiration dripped into his collar. He loosened his tie. He thumped the Bible with loud whacks.

It's kind of like a devil dance, Molly thought. At once she was shocked at her own wickedness. She stole a look at Mother. But Mother had pulled down her veil, so Molly couldn't see her eyes. Daddy sat like a stone, staring straight ahead. Kate caught Molly's eye and tried to smile.

Suddenly, as if someone had slammed a door, the sermon stopped. For a minute no one dared breathe. Even the baby was quiet. The preacher turned to Molly.

"Play, Sister, play!" he commanded. "Something to soothe the weary soul."

Molly fumbled for her music and began the "Funeral March." It sounded all wrong on the organ. Notes ran into each other, muddled and soupy. When one pedal stuck, the music skipped a beat.

She looked up to see what was happening. What she saw made Molly forget all about the pedals. Someone had lifted the lid of the long pine box! Mourners were shuffling by for one last look at Maggie Corn. Molly had sometimes dreamed about Death. Now it was only three steps away.

What was it like to be dead? What did Mrs. Corn's body look like? Oh, she could never in all the world stare at someone who was dead. Faster now, even a little wildly, Molly pumped the pedals and pressed the white keys. Thank goodness, she had a job to do. No one would expect her to look.

Still, from her place at the organ, Molly watched the Corn family. They walked slowly by the pine box. Some faces were hard and cold. Nell sobbed loudly and had to be led. Old Mr. Corn leaned on one of his sons. He seemed to be in a fog. One by one, the littlest children were lifted up for a last look at their great-granny. Molly wondered how much they understood about Death. How much did she herself understand, or even want to understand?

Preacher Boggs pressed a heavy hand on each passing shoulder. "Amen, Brother!" and "Lean on the Lord, Sister!" he told them.

Next came the congregation. Each woman carried a bunch of ugly crêpe paper roses with long wire stems. Some were set in glass fruit jars. The roses were bright red and yellow and pink. Mountain women

sold them on the street in Ducktown on Saturdays. Today the sad-eyed women set the ugly flowers around the box in which Maggie Corn was sleeping.

Molly flipped the pages of the hymnbook and began playing number 73. It was called "In the Sweet Bye and Bye." Preacher Boggs nodded at her, then waved for everyone to sing.

In the middle of the second verse, Maggie gasped. Kate was coming down the church aisle, bringing their pansy wreath! Molly had forgotten all about their flowers, the only real ones in the church. Her hands began to tremble. Twice she played a wrong chord. She watched Kate from the corner of one eye. Would Kate dare look at Mrs. Corn's dead body? How *could* she do it?

Molly needn't have wondered, for of course Kate dared. With a stiff face, she followed the other mourners. She set the pansy wreath among the paper flowers. Without a quiver, Kate took a long look into the pine box. Then she walked quickly back to sit with her father.

Would this funeral never end? Already it seemed like a mournful dream that didn't know when to fade.

"Amen! Amen!" Preacher Boggs shouted, when the last of the hill people had straggled by. His voice was by now as rusty as his coat.

"Brethren and Sistern!" he croaked. "Be ye not sorrowful. Just like the Bible has done told us, we'll meet Sister Corn on that heavenly shore. Now sing with me, everybody—that wonderful old hymn, number seven."

So they sang, almost in tune and faster than before:

Yes, we'll gather by the river,
The beautiful, the beautiful river,
Gather with the saints at the river
That flows by the throne of God.

"Hallelujah! Amen!" Preacher Boggs bowed his head.

"Amen! Amen!" came an echo from every corner of the church.

Someone closed the pine box with a thud. Someone else piled the paper flowers on its top. Eight mountain men lifted it to their shoulders and carried Maggie Corn from the church.

This was no time to cry, Molly knew. How could she see the music through tears? Besides, Kate hadn't cried, even when she looked at Mrs. Corn dead.

People followed the pine box. Molly played number 17. It was called "Beulah Land." Maggie had heard Mrs. Corn singing it to herself in a cracked and quavering voice when she thought no one was listening. The hymn had a nice melody. If only the organ didn't whine so.

The last mourner shuffled out. One red paper rose lay forgotten in the aisle. All was quiet, like a lull after a summer storm. Molly closed the organ. The music had been awful, she admitted to herself, though she had done her best.

Daddy came quickly toward her. He gave Molly a bear hug.

"I'm proud of you, honey," he said. "Now let's go home—fast! Why don't you ask Kate to ride with us and stay for supper?"

Mother lifted her veil and kissed Molly. She said not a word. But she gave Molly a long, gentle look, then turned to Daddy.

"I told you, William, that this whole thing was not a good idea. The child is stricken. Just look at her eyes."

Then they were in the car.

"What did she look like?" Molly whispered to Kate as they rode home in the back seat. "Was it perfectly *awful* to see someone dead?"

"She never looked half so nice before," Kate whispered back. "She had on your mother's old blue dress, the one with a white collar—and it was clean. Her poor wrinkled hands were folded. She looked rested, Maggie Corn did. She needed rest. I'm kind of glad she died."

Molly was shocked. But when she thought of Kate's words, they made a kind of sense. Mrs. Corn's life had been so hard. Maybe she needed the long sleep that people call Death. Heaven (Beulah Land, mountain people called it), would be a happier home than Maggie Corn had ever dreamed of.

"They're going to bury her beside little Johnny," she told Kate. "You remember, the one who's 'dangling his little feet around the throne of God.' Next summer let's take some *real* flowers to put on both their graves—instead of those awful paper things."

Daddy must have been listening.

"All right, girls," he said cheerfully, his voice no longer hushed and solemn. "That's enough about Death and funerals. I know what I intend to do after supper. Ruthie and I are going to beat a certain pair of young ladies to a frazzle in a hot game of Parchesi."

The two girls gave each other their secret look, not

meant for parents. Daddy and Ruth had been trying for perfect ages. But they would never beat Molly and Kate in a Parchesi game—not in a hundred years. They would make sure of that.

12

SILVER MEDALS

"Here's something that might please you," Daddy said. He pulled the mail from his pocket and gave a long envelope to Molly. It had *St. Nicholas* magazine printed in one corner.

Molly ripped it open. Inside, the letter said,

> Dear Molly,
>
> The editors of *St. Nicholas* magazine have awarded you a silver medal for your poem, "Fire on the Mountain." Congratulations! The poem will be printed in a later issue of our magazine. It will appear on the "St. Nicholas League Page," with work of other young people.
>
> May this award encourage you to continue your writing.
>
> With our good wishes,
> the Editors

It couldn't be true! A letter from real editors? Molly read it again. A tiny package was glued to one corner. Her fingers fumbled, trying to unwrap it. Inside was a real silver medal the size of a quarter, with a pin on the back. A band of deep blue and the words "The St. Nicholas League" circled its edge. There was a little red, white, and blue banner enameled in the middle.

Mother glanced up from her sewing, then stared.

"What on earth's the matter, dear?" she asked. "You're trembling! Have you had bad news?"

"Oh, Mother, look! My poem won a silver medal from *St. Nicholas*."

Then there was a real hubbub. The whole family had to hear "Fire on the Mountain" read aloud. With happy tears in her eyes, Mother hugged Molly hard.

"I rather suspected we had a young poet in our family," Daddy said proudly.

Even Ruthie was impressed.

"I'm going to send *St. Nicholas* one of my pictures," she decided. "Maybe they'll give me a silver medal, too." Ruth was going to be an artist. Her watercolors of rabbits and elves and flowers were as real as anything. So were her pictures of owls and windmills.

When she saw the pin, even Vashti was pleased and proud.

"I ain't never thought much of pomes," she said. "Even reading 'em makes girls too dreamylike to be much use to anybody. But that there fire on the mountain do look like a snake sometimes. Do snakes be some kind of dragon?"

That night Molly read the poem to Penny for a bedtime story. She read it slowly, three times. Penny didn't understand it, of course, but she listened. Penny would like it if Molly read her the dictionary. That was one of the good things about very little sisters. They loved their older sisters, even if one of them was too proud for her own good.

Molly pinned her medal on the lining of her jewelry box. Now she must write that poem about the woods in snow. Maybe someday she would win a *St. Nicholas* gold medal. Then she would know she was really a poet.

She couldn't decide whether to tell Kate or not. It might look like bragging to show her the silver pin. Maybe she would let Kate read the poem when it was published. Seeing Molly's name in print in a real magazine might make Kate stop laughing at people who wrote poetry. Right this minute she must write Cousin Eva the news about the silver medal.

Molly had written only the first sentence when the phone rang. It was Kate. She sounded excited and out of breath.

"You know that hill just back of the schoolhouse? There's a dog howling on top, where the old Burra Burra mine shaft is. It's been howling all morning. My daddy says he heard it in the middle of the night. It kept him awake."

"What of it?" Molly asked. Dogs howled whenever they felt like it.

Kate paid no attention.

"I'll meet you at the footbridge over Little Potato Creek in five minutes. We've got to find out what's the matter with that dog." She hung up before Molly could say another word.

If there was one solid rule in Isabella Camp, it was "*Never* go near an abandoned mine shaft!" These shafts were holes, like deep wells, dug long ago by men hoping to find copper. They were dotted here and there among the hills. If no copper ore was found, mine shafts were forgotten. Each had a wire fence around it. Every Isabella child knew there was danger in going near that fence. The edge of the hole might cave in. Some of the old shafts were hundreds of feet deep.

The girls met on the footbridge.

"Hurry!" Kate was flushed and wild with excitement. "Maybe there's somebody down in that old Burra Burra mine shaft. Maybe the dog knows it. It might be his master."

"Silly!" Molly replied calmly. Who was being silly this time? "Nobody ever goes up that hill. Why would they? There's nothing on it except a lot of gullies. Everybody with a grain of sense stays away from old mine shafts."

"Come on!" Kate insisted. "We've got to find out what's making that dog howl all day. Nobody else will, if we don't."

Well, it would be an adventure, anyway. Molly had never seen Kate so excited. The girls began to run. At the schoolyard gate they stopped for breath, because Molly had a stitch in her side and her socks had slid down to her ankles.

From here they could see the hill with the Burra Burra shaft on its top. There, outlined against the sky, was the fence. There was the dog, too. Its head was thrown back, and it was still howling. The mournful sound drifted down to the girls.

"It's a hound dog," Kate said. Nothing in the world is as sorrowful as the howl of a hound. Though the sun was shining brightly, Molly shivered. Could Kate's guess be true? Suppose there might really be a man down that deserted shaft? It might even be a hillbilly boy. A girl would have more sense than to climb that particular hill at all, for any reason. Besides, what girl ever had a hound dog for a pet?

She and Kate were climbing now. It had rained hard yesterday, so the bare red clay was slick. The girls kept slipping. Once Molly slid into a deep gully. Kate fished her out. Molly's right knee was skinned, but it bled only a little. One more skinned knee didn't matter much. Both girls were now muddy from top to toe. Molly knew Mother wouldn't like it that her second-best middy blouse was streaked with clay, but by this time she was almost as excited as Kate. There must be some reason for that dog's howls.

Then she thought of something that caught her breath.

"Wait a minute!" she called to Kate, who was a few steps ahead. "Suppose it's a mad dog. We'd better be careful."

Kate didn't even reply. She kept climbing. Here the gullies were smaller and the slope was less steep. At last they neared the crest of the hill.

Suddenly Molly exclaimed in surprise, "Why, that's old Mike Malloon's dog! I saw it just last Saturday when Mike came begging at our back door. Mother gave him a big, thick ham sandwich and some apples. She won't give tramps money because they might spend it on vanilla." Mountain people drank whole bottles of vanilla sometimes, because cake flavoring had lots of alcohol in it. It was cheaper than moonshine whiskey.

"Are you sure it's the same dog?" Kate asked. "Hounds look a lot alike."

"Yes, I'm sure. It looked half-starved then, like it does now."

The girls drew nearer. The poor creature kept right on howling in long, mournful cries. Ribs showed through its skin like the bones of a skeleton.

"I wish we knew its name," Kate said. "Here, dog! Here, dog!" she called gently. The hound paid no attention. It didn't even turn its head to look at Molly and Kate.

"We should have brought some food with us," Molly said. "The poor thing is hungry. Maybe that's why it howls."

"Then why doesn't it howl outside somebody's back door?" Kate asked sensibly. Boldly, she went nearer.

"What if it was old Mike Malloon who fell down that mine shaft in the night?" Molly shuddered. "I don't dare go near the fence to look down."

"Neither do I," Kate agreed. "We couldn't see in that dark hole anyway. But we can walk around it, not too close, if we're careful."

So they did. The fence was old and neglected. Some of the posts leaned at a tipsy angle. Here and there the wire sagged. Because it was so far from any road or path, no one had inspected the fence in goodness knows when.

Suddenly Kate shouted, "Look what I've found!" She picked up a small empty box. "Hill-Billy Snuff" was printed on its cover in red and green letters. "If this had been out in yesterday's rain, it would be faded and soggy by now."

Molly gasped.

"Do you really think—?"

"Yes," Kate said firmly. "Now I'm sure there's a man down in there. It was a dark night, and he fell over that low part of the fence. The box fell out of his pocket. Look! There's a footprint in the clay."

Yes, there was the print of a man-sized shoe, just this side of the sagging wire. What a detective Kate was! A real-live Sherlock Holmes.

In the silences between the dog's howls, the girls began to shout, "Hello! Hello!" They shouted until they were hoarse. They strained their ears, hoping to hear a faint voice rise from the bottom of the mine shaft.

There was no answer—only the faraway caw of a crow in the valley behind them.

"We've got to get help," Kate decided. The hound had noticed them at last. It stopped howling and was now licking their shoes. Its tail waved weakly, and there was a pleading look in its bleary eyes.

"You stay here," Kate said firmly, "so the hound will know somebody is doing something. Maybe it won't howl anymore. I'll run home as quick as lightning and phone Captain Jim. He'll know what to do."

So Kate began half-running, half-sliding down the hillside. Though the spring sun was warm and there was no wind, Molly shivered. It was an eerie feeling, being left alone with a strange dog and maybe a dead man down Burra Burra mine shaft. Maybe the man wasn't dead, but just asleep. Or maybe he was too deep underground to hear their shouts.

Molly sat on a large rock. The restless hound ran back and forth, between her feet and the fence. Kate's figure grew smaller; then she disappeared around the curve of the hill. Soon she would reach home and telephone.

But what if Captain Jim didn't listen to her story? Grown-ups often paid no attention to children. What would she and Kate do then? Even Daddy might think their tale of a man down the old mine shaft a crazy notion. Didn't hound dogs howl for no reason at all, whenever they felt like it? But a snuffbox, dry after a heavy rain, ought to prove that something serious had happened.

Time crept like a slow river in flatlands. Today Molly couldn't enjoy watching shadows chase each other on distant hills. She couldn't play at imagining that the high clouds above her were billowy shapes of elephants or camels with three humps. Even Angellico Mountain in the east and Big Frog in the west didn't seem their usual friendly selves.

Had Kate been gone an hour? Maybe two? The sun was past noon in the sky. No wonder she was hungry. She had missed lunch. How worried Mother would be!

Then Molly remembered the man down the mine shaft. If he was really there, he had had no food for hours and hours. Neither had his dog. Surely Kate would remember to bring food when she came back. When would that be? And would she bring help?

Just as she was despairing, Molly saw a cluster of figures come around the bend of the hill. Her heart leapt, for, besides the little shape that was Kate, she counted five tall ones. All carried loads on their backs. For the first time, Molly patted the nervous hound.

"Don't worry," she told it. "Somebody's coming to help your master—if it *is* your master down that hole."

As they climbed, the shapes became men: Captain Jim and four of his mine workers. With them, of course, was Kate. Molly waved joyfully to her.

At last the rescue party reached the top of the hill.

"So you two girls think you've solved the mystery about that blasted howling dog," Captain Jim said gruffly. He wasn't teasing. His face looked serious. Kate had remembered to bring food for the hound. It nibbled with only half a heart, then ran from one man to another with eager yelps.

"I brought some crackers and an orange in my pocket, too," Kate told Molly in a low voice. "In case they really find a man down there. If they do, he's bound to be starved."

The men set to work. The loads on their backs were coils of rope and cable, a first-aid chest, and a folding stretcher. So Captain Jim had believed there must be some truth in their story. A thick rope was tied around one man's waist. Three men held its other end and lowered him down the mine shaft. Slowly, slowly, he disappeared. He was gone for a time that seemed forever. No one spoke. Even the hound was quiet. Not even a crow cawed from the valley.

At last, from far, far away (surely it was the middle of the earth), there came a faint shout.

"It's a man, all right!"

At that, Captain Jim fell flat on the ground. Inside the fence he slithered dangerously close to the edge of the hole.

"Steady!" he called. "We'll send down a cable to pull him up with. Is he dead or alive?"

"I don't know," came the thin voice.

They threw down the heavy cable. After a long time there came the call, "Ready! Pull him up!" Which the other men did, slowly, slowly.

Molly and Kate held each other tightly and almost wished they were far away. Could they dare look, Molly wondered? What would a dead man be like?

"Easy does it!" Captain Jim shouted to the men who were pulling hard on the ropes and cable. Just then a lolling head appeared over the edge of the mine shaft. It looked like a limp doll with no stuffing. Then came a body and dangling legs. No one breathed. Was the man dead or alive? One thing was sure. It was Mike Malloon.

Captain Jim listened to his heart for a long minute.

At last he shouted, "He's alive, all right! Put him on the stretcher. Easy there, men!"

Kate and Molly hugged each other for joy. Though the poor man certainly didn't look it, he was alive.

"We might as well eat these crackers and the orange ourselves," Kate said, as the girls followed the men with the stretcher down the hill. "Mike Malloon can't eat them now. And we missed our lunch."

Once home there was a real hullabaloo. The Tyler and Meade families were as proud as peacocks. Molly and Kate felt like heroines in an adventure book. Their adventure had had a storybook ending, too. For the doctor said poor old Mike Malloon would live. He had a broken leg, but that would heal.

He was now in the company hospital, being fed broth and tea. He wouldn't have to beg any more. Captain Jim had promised the tramp a job cleaning his office when he was strong enough. And the dog (its name was Rip) lay beside its master's bed, well fed and no longer howling.

That should have ended the story, though it didn't. In the next Saturday's Atlanta paper, there was a headline on page four. In large black type it said:

TWO GIRLS AND DOG
SAVE MAN FROM DESERTED MINE SHAFT

Under it, in smaller print, was the whole story, with Kate's and Molly's names. Two weeks later, letters came for both girls. They were from the president of the Copper Company. The two silver medals tucked inside were exactly alike.

For days both girls tried to look modest. So did their parents. Not many daughters had won such honors. But, deep inside, Molly was a little troubled. She and Kate hadn't pulled poor old Mr. Malloon from the mine shaft all by themselves. Still, if they hadn't given the alarm, he might have died down that awful hole. Maybe Rip deserved the medals more. Or maybe Kate should have had one, for it had been her idea to investigate the mystery of the howling dog.

Molly pinned her life-saving medal to the lining of

her jewelry box, beside the poetry pin. She was tempted to tell Kate this wasn't her only silver medal. Yet somehow she didn't quite have the heart to brag just now. Maybe she would tell Kate on the day when "Fire on the Mountain" was printed in *St. Nicholas* magazine.

13

GRADUATION

Mother stopped Molly in the middle of the C-sharp major scale.

"When you finish practising, dear, won't you and Ruth make some sugar cookies? Miss Alice and Mrs. Tyler are coming for tea tomorrow."

"Oh, goody!" Molly was pleased. Miss Alice almost never had time to visit the homes of her Isabella School pupils. "May Ruthie and Kate and I have tea with you?"

"You may pass sandwiches and cookies," Mother said. "After that, you girls must leave us. We ladies have something important to discuss. Now finish your practising, dear. I love that Schubert 'Serenade' you're learning."

What on earth did the two mothers and Miss Alice have to discuss? She and Kate never had trouble with their schoolwork. All four parents were happy with their grades. Of course, last month Kate had made 91 in arithmetic, while her grade had been only 86. That was because decimals were so hard. But then, Molly's composition grade made up for it by being a point or two higher than Kate's. No, there was no trouble about grades. Next month (Molly had promised herself) she would master decimals. If Kate could do it, so could she.

Now her fingers practised by themselves. At the end of half an hour Molly had played all the major scales, three exercises in the Czerny book, and two pages of "Serenade." All the while her thoughts had been on the tea party, not on the music. It was almost as if her fingers had brains inside themselves. Imagining a little brain in each finger, Molly giggled to herself.

Making cookies was always fun-work. Molly and Ruth had the kitchen all to themselves on this Friday afternoon. By the time they had opened the cookbook and found the recipe, Penny burst through the swinging door.

"I want to help," she announced. Of course, Penny's "help" was really a bother. But Molly remembered "cooking" when she was little. Making real cookies was a hundred times more fun than mixing sandpile mud cakes. Besides, bits off real cookie dough could be snitched and tasted when no one was looking.

So they let Penny sift the flour. She spilled only a little on the floor. Ruth creamed the butter with a wooden spoon. Molly beat the eggs until they turned yellow, then greased the cookie sheets.

The best part, of course, was rolling out the dough. Molly and Penny used cookie cutters. Ruth, who was

going to be an artist when she grew up, cut pretty shapes of birds and fishes with a pastry knife. After the cookies were baked, the girls trimmed them with currants and sprinkles of red sugar. The big girls praised Penny's cookies, though they were weird, lumpy shapes. They also smiled at each other over her curly head. For Penny had red sugar on her nose and flour up to her elbows.

For the tea party next day, Miss Alice wore her best lace collar and her string of crystal beads. Kate came to help pass teacups and cookies. Penny passed the lemon slices. If spilled, they wouldn't make much of a mess.

"Thank you, girls," Mother said at last. "Now run along while we three ladies have our chat."

Kate was as curious as Molly. The two girls sat in the window seat of the playroom. They began a game of

Mah-Jongg with Ruth, though nobody had much heart for it.

"I'd like to know what's so secret!" Kate exploded at last. "I'm sure it's about us. We're old enough to know what they're saying, whatever it is."

They had to "possess their souls with patience," which was one of Mother's favorite sayings. After supper she and Daddy had their own private talk in the library. At last they called Molly to join them.

"We're thinking about your next school year." Daddy looked serious. "You and Kate ought, by rights, to be in the seventh grade."

Molly already knew that. What was there to "think about"? Why did her parents look so solemn? Then Mother spoke up.

"You and Kate should be in a class with boys and girls besides each other. Mrs. Tyler and I have thought so for a long while. Miss Alice agrees with us."

Molly was surprised.

"But there isn't anybody our age in Isabella Camp," she exclaimed, Everyone knew that. Other Camp children were babies, in the fourth grade and below.

"You girls are entirely too young to go away to school," Daddy said then. "So Miss Alice has spoken with the principal of the Ducktown School. He has agreed to let you and Kate graduate with his seventh-grade class in May. Then, in September, you'll enter high school with Ducktown children."

"But we're only in the sixth grade now!" Molly was shocked. Somehow she and Kate had never thought much about what came next. *Now* was what was important.

"Miss Alice thinks you both ought to skip seventh grade," Mother told her. "She thinks you should be studying Latin and algebra next year. She says you need a challenge and a chance to make new friends besides each other."

Molly was stunned. It would take time to digest the whole idea.

Just then the phone rang. It was Kate, of course. She had been told the news, too.

"I can't believe it!" Kate said in a voice that didn't sound at all like hers. "I'm kind of scared to skip a grade, aren't you? My sister says Latin and algebra are hard."

It was something new to hear that Kate was scared of anything.

"Miss Alice says we need a challenge," Molly replied firmly. She could at least pretend to be braver than Kate. "If she thinks we can do it, we can."

After that, life grew complicated. Miss Alice began giving the girls more homework.

"Let's be sure you're prepared for advanced mathematics," she said. "You'd better write two compositions a week, too, instead of one. Three hundred words each." So there was less time for fun. Also, Mr. Gray, the Ducktown School principal, had asked Molly and Kate to play a piano duet on graduation night.

"Schubert's 'Marche Militaire' is just the thing," Miss Julie decided. "The seventh-grade class will march to the stage while you play it. Then you two girls will take places beside them and receive your certificates."

Duets were fun to play, but a problem. Which girl should play the treble part? It carried the melody. It was exciting both to play and to listen to. The bass part was just a dull *thump, thump* that sounded easier than it was. Nobody would pay any attention to it.

"You must draw straws," Miss Julie decided. So they did. Naturally Kate picked the short straw, which meant she would play treble. Kate didn't exactly crow about it, but she couldn't help looking as pleased as the cat that once swallowed the canary. Molly tossed her head as if it didn't matter, though of course it did. Everyone would think she couldn't play the piano half as well as Kate.

"I'll have to make you a new white dress," Mother said. "Voile, I think. And a bertha collar would hide your thin shoulders, dear. I'll scallop the hem of the skirt and put lace on it."

"May I wear the blue satin sash you've been saving for something special?" Molly asked. The sash was beautiful, the color of a robin's egg. Kate was to wear her big sister's white dress. Being the oldest sister had its good points, Molly thought. She didn't have to wear hand-me-downs that often didn't fit.

On the Saturday before Graduation Night, Molly and Kate practised the "Marche Militaire" on the stage piano at Ducktown School. They hoped no one would notice that it was out of tune. Two notes in the bass didn't even sound.

After Isabella School's large room with its bright walls and pictures, Ducktown School looked dark and plain. It was big, with two floors and lots of classrooms. Their footsteps echoed as they walked down the empty halls. The auditorium was enormous, or so the girls thought. It had seats for one hundred people and a stage with a red curtain. What would it be like on Graduation Night? All those seats would be filled with strange people. Already Kate looked a little pale, which meant she was maybe a little scared, too.

What would Ducktown girls be like? She had never met any. There would be boys her own age, too. At the thought Molly's heart skipped a beat. It would be strange to have boys in class. Would they be miles ahead of her in math? It was bad enough to keep up with Kate in decimals. Most of all, would Ducktown children think she and Kate were snooty? Their fathers were officials in the Copper Company. Fathers of Ducktown boys and girls were mine and smelter workers.

Between extra homework and trying on the new dress and practising the duet with Kate, days flew by as quickly as the flash of a firefly. At last it was the tenth of May—Graduation Night. The new white dress was lovely. As Mother had promised, it had a scalloped skirt trimmed with lace and a wide collar like a little cape.

She was the last to be ready. Molly brushed her hair an extra hundred strokes, to make it shine under the stage lights. She looked at herself in Mother's long mirror. Her right knee, as usual, had an ugly scab, and both knees were bony. Otherwise she was almost pretty, she told herself. It was time to go. Daddy was honking the car's horn by the back gate.

Suddenly Molly ran back to her dresser. She unlocked her jewelry box with its secret key and took out the two silver medals. Quickly she pinned one on each side of her petticoat, where they wouldn't show.

When they reached Ducktown School, Kate was already there. At the stage door she grabbed Molly and clung to her. Her white dress, Molly noticed, was the right length for once. It ended, like Molly's, just above her knees, which were round and dimpled, as knees ought to be. Still, something was wrong.

"Wait 'til you see the others!" she whispered urgently in Molly's ear. "They're not children like us. They make me feel *young*, and I was twelve last month. You and I don't belong at Ducktown School." Kate was pale and her freckles brighter than ever. She was shaking like an aspen leaf in a whiff of wind. What on earth was she talking about?

Molly peeped with Kate through a crack in the red curtain. Ducktown School's seventh grade was sitting in the front row of the crowded auditorium. Kate was right. All twenty of them looked old, like teenagers. Maybe some of them were really already in their teens. One girl even had what Mother called a "figure." The boys wore long pants and ties. The girls' skirts were shocking. These hung halfway to their ankles, like skirts of real young ladies. And every single girl was wearing heels and long silk stockings!

"One of those girls has on lipstick!" Molly said in shocked tones. "And earrings! They're like little girls playing dress-up." This time she clutched Kate. "They'll think we're babies!" Molly heard her own voice tremble nervously.

"I have an idea," Kate said. "Take off your socks."

"Why on earth would you say such a thing?" Molly was shocked.

"Because then our knees won't look so bare. People might even think we have on silk stockings. Come on! Do it fast!"

Maybe Kate was right. So both girls took off their silk knee socks. Mary Janes felt stiff and funny with bare feet in them.

"Now untie that big bow of your sash," Kate ordered. "Your dress looks older without it." Her own dress had no sash to begin with. It broke Molly's heart to hide the beautiful blue watered-silk sash behind the door with their socks. But Kate was right. Now they felt—perhaps they even looked—a little older.

"You're awfully pale," Molly dared to tell Kate.

"So are you," Kate retorted. "We'll look like ghosts under those stage lights when we play our duet."

Just then Miss Julie breezed in to wish them well. Kate had another thought. That was one good thing about her, Molly had to admit. Kate often had good ideas in a pinch.

"Please, may Molly and I wear a little of your lipstick, just this once? It will be like wearing makeup for a play."

Miss Julie hesitated.

"You girls do look a little white," she decide at last. "Yes, I'll put a bit of pink on your lips, though I wonder what your mothers will say."

It was time for the "Marche Militaire." The bare legs felt daring. Still, it was the lipstick that gave them courage to walk to the piano.

Glare from the footlights was like a bright screen between the girls and the audience. Molly was glad she couldn't see the shocked faces of her family. What would Mother and Daddy think of no knee socks and no sash? Maybe from a distance they wouldn't notice the lipstick. For a minute she forgot the scab on her right knee. Now, instead of being pale, she noticed, Kate's face was red as a beet.

In spite of everything, they played well. Those little finger brains were hard at work, Molly thought in a flash. The march, though, became a gallop. For Kate played faster and faster. Try as she did to hold her partner back, Molly had to follow the lead of the treble.

Then the duet was over, with no wrong notes to hurt anybody's ears. The audience clapped in a roar. Both girls bobbed little curtsies. Too late, Molly wondered what girls should do when they were too old for curtsies. Would their new classmates laugh at them?

The other graduates had marched up to the stage. They now sat in a row of chairs. Kate grabbed her hand. Then she and Molly sank into the last two seats. The rest was like a dream. A large man in a striped suit made a speech. Later Molly couldn't remember a word of it. Though she pulled at her skirt every now and then, it wouldn't stretch to cover her bare knees. Her mouth felt funny, wearing lipstick for the first time. She glanced sideways at Kate, who was staring straight ahead, stiff as a poker.

At last it was time for the certificates, which were tied with blue and gold streamers. One by one, Ducktown School's principal read the class list. One by one the boys and girls walked across the stage in answer to their names. Then it was their turn. Who would have to go first, she or Kate? For once Molly hoped Kate would be ahead of her.

The principal looked at them and smiled. Perhaps he wasn't stiff and stern. Maybe he was really a nice man, though any man teacher would take some getting used to.

"Now we have two little ladies," he said, "who come to our class from Isabella School: Kate Tyler and Molly Meade. They will join us at Ducktown High in September. Will you come forward, girls? I am sure the other members of your class will welcome you."

The audience clapped politely. The twenty other boys and girls stared at Molly and Kate curiously. They did not applaud. Two girls whispered to each other. A boy tittered. Not one smiled.

I can't walk past them all alone, Molly thought wildly. I simply can't. She felt glued to her chair. Kate looked as if she might faint any minute. Kate faint? It was unheard of. But so was everything else.

Then the principal saved their lives.

"Will you two girls come together for your certificates?" he asked kindly. In a flash, Molly knew she was going to like her first man teacher.

Forgetting that they probably looked like little girls, she and Kate walked past their new classmates. They even held hands, Molly remembered later. Mr. Gray smiled and gave one certificate to Kate, one to Molly. This time they knew better than to curtsy. Instead, like the others, they shook hands with the principal and returned to their seats. They found their voices in time to sing the "Star-Spangled Banner" with everyone else. Graduation was over.

Not quite. When the curtain went down, their new classmates began chattering to each other. A few stared boldly and curiously at Molly and Kate. As if we were strange fish or birds, Molly thought. Two boys laughed rudely. No one spoke to them at all.

"I don't call that much of a welcome," Kate said finally. Then their families came backstage. There was a flurry of kisses and congratulations. In the excitement, Molly and Kate even kissed each other.

"That was the worst hour of my whole life," Kate admitted the next day. She and Molly were sprawling on the playroom floor. They had locked the door to keep out curious little ears.

"Were you as scared as I was?" Molly asked, though she already knew the answer. She would never forget Kate's face when that awful boy stared and tittered at them. Today she felt very close to Kate.

"I thought I'd die if I had to walk across that stage all by myself," Kate admitted. "It was easier, going together. Do you think we'll like Latin? And will any of those stuck-up boys and girls ever speak to us? I guess we'd better stick together, in case they don't."

That was exactly what Molly had been thinking.

"Was your mother upset about our bare legs and the lipstick?" Kate asked.

"She didn't say a word," Molly told her. "Not even about the missing sash. Do you suppose mothers really remember what it was like to be girls like us?"

"I wouldn't be surprised," Kate said. "I'll tell you a secret," she confided to Molly. "You mustn't ever tell anybody. I wore my life-saving medal under my dress, where it wouldn't show."

"So did I!" Molly said in amazement. "Pinned to my petticoat, so it wouldn't look like bragging."

They hugged each other. Imagine both doing the very same thing in secret.

Molly didn't say a word about the *St. Nicholas* medal. It didn't seem right somehow. Kate might never need to know that she was going to be a poet someday. Friends didn't have to spend their whole lives rivaling each other. They didn't always have to do the same things well.

Kate jumped to her feet.

"Come on! Let's find the little girls and play Prisoners' Base with them. I'm sick of being a 'young lady,' aren't you? I choose you for my side."

Kate dashed outdoors in her harum-scarum way.

This time they were on the same team, Molly thought happily. Ducktown High School was going to be frightening. Maybe she and Kate could survive it together when September came.

MOTHER'S MERINGUES

Making meringues is easy with an electric mixer. Vashti had to beat egg whites and sugar with a hand egg beater. Sometimes Molly took a turn, until her arm felt that it might drop off. But meringues are so delicious that neither she nor Vashti really minded all that effort.

INGREDIENTS

- 1 teaspoon vanilla extract
- 1 teaspoon cider vinegar
- 1 teaspoon water
- 4 egg whites
- ½ teaspoon baking powder
- ⅛ teaspoon salt
- 1 cup of granulated sugar that has been sifted through a flour sifter to remove lumps
- margarine to grease cookie sheet

1. Preheat oven to 250° F.
2. Grease cookie sheet and line with smooth brown paper.
3. Mix vanilla, vinegar, and water in a small cup.
4. In a large mixing bowl, beat egg whites with baking powder and salt until there are soft peaks.
5. Gradually add 1 tablespoon of sugar at a time, alternately with a few drops of the liquid. When only sugar is left, continue adding gradually. Beat all the while.
6. When the ingredients are all added, continue beating until mixture is very thick and glossy.
7. Drop the meringues from a large spoon, making about 12 mounds on paper-lined cookie sheet.
8. Bake for about an hour, until the meringues are crusty, but not brown.
9. Remove them from paper with a spatula and let cool.
10. Serve with chocolate sauce or mashed strawberries and whipped cream.

ABOUT THE AUTHOR

HELEN REEDER CROSS spent her childhood in Isabella, Tennessee; she now lives in Larchmont, New York.

A graduate of Duke University, with an M.A. from Trinity College, the author specializes in the study of the nineteenth century, and her books, *Life in Lincoln's America*, *A Curiosity for the Curious*, and *The Real Tom Thumb*, reflect this interest. She taught at the Masters School in Dobbs Ferry, New York, for many years before retiring to devote more time to her own writing—and to teaching courses at Westchester Community College, attending chamber music concerts, taking nature walks, painting with watercolors, cooking gourmet meals (using some of Mother's recipes), and enjoying her grandchildren and their friends.

ABOUT THE ARTIST

CATHERINE STOCK is a free-lance artist who has lived in many of the world's great cities. She has illustrated such lovely books as *The Royal Gift, Princess & Pumpkin*, and her own *Christmas Angel Collection*.